# CAP

Northerner Cap Millet, hunting for his wife's murderers, agrees to take charge of a cattle drive to Abilene for his former boss. Arriving with a negro, Millet runs into opposition from the Texan cowboys. But Millet has a way with himself, which can overcome the resentment, deliver the herd safely and track down his wife's killers.

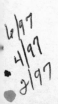

*Books by Jim Bowden*
*in the Linford Western Library:*

SHOWDOWN IN SALT FORK

# JIM BOWDEN

◆

# CAP

*Complete and Unabridged*

# LINFORD
*Leicester*

First published in Great Britain in 1978 by
Robert Hale Limited
London

First Linford Edition
published September 1991

British Library CIP Data

Bowden, Jim *1923 –*
  Cap. – Large print ed. –
  Linford western library
  I. Title
  823.914

  ISBN 0–7089–7089–3

Published by
F. A. Thorpe (Publishing) Ltd.
Anstey, Leicestershire
Set by Words & Graphics Ltd.
Anstey, Leicestershire
Printed and bound in Great Britain by
T. J. Press (Padstow) Ltd., Padstow, Cornwall

# 1

JOHNNY HINES stirred on the bench outside the bunk-house. His tall, lean figure straightened. The movement disturbed the Hash Knife cowboys who lazed in the shade, seeking some respite from the heat of the Texas sun. They glanced at their foreman. Johnny was alert; his eyes, beating through the distance, tried to identify the three riders who had broken the skyline of the rise a mile to the east. The cowboys followed his gaze. They stiffened. Their waiting was over.

The door of the bunk-house creaked, sending a ripple of disturbance through the silent tension which had come with the sighting of the three horsemen. A whisper, and those men who had chosen to lounge on their bunks stepped outside and stared at the three distant figures.

Johnny sensed the tension heighten and knew that the resentment, felt by the men he bossed, had boiled to the surface again.

They were loyal and he thanked them for it. He reckoned, like they did, that he could boss their first cattle drive north, but their employer, Frank Peters, had decided to bring in an outsider. There had been murmuring, even talk of them refusing to go, but Johnny had persuaded them otherwise.

The boss needed this drive to be successful and in consequence their jobs were dependent on it. Johnny knew the whole outfit would follow him through hell-fire with a few rustlers, Comanches, Arapahoes, Cheyennes and Sioux thrown in. He had asked them to do the same for the new man. Reluctantly they had agreed and, even though he could not get rid of their resentment towards the newcomer, they respected his loyalty to the boss.

Johnny had come to the Hash Knife when Frank Peters had returned four years ago after the war between states.

The longhorns had multiplied during the hostilities and hundreds of thousands roamed the Texas plains. There was a surplus of cattle with no ready market. The big demand, in the north, was thousands of miles away. The cattle were in the wrong place.

Then last year, in 1868, cattle were driven from way down near San Antonio, following an old trail used by Jesse Chisholm, a Cherokee trader, to the markets in the north. It was a daring idea but it worked, and now Frank Peters figured the Hash Knife could do the same.

But he was bringing in a stranger to boss the drive. He had broken the news to his men yesterday, when he had returned from town, telling them that the stranger's name was Cap Millet, that he knew him personally, that he was good with cattle, horses and men and was hired for this one drive only.

The Hash Knife riders figured that with a name like Cap he must have been a captain with the Confederates, so it really hit their guts when Frank revealed that Millet had been a captain in the Union Army.

Resentment was there in a flash and it seemed as if the bunk-house would explode, but Frank stamped his authority on the gathering immediately and gave his reason for bringing in a Yankee to boss the drive instead of Johnny.

Frank figured they might run into trouble up north. The war was not long gone and the war still rankled in men's minds. Johnny saw his point, for his riders were all from the south.

Johnny was one of those who took the view that the war was over and done with and everyone should get on with living together in a peaceable way. But Johnny wasn't hit by the war like some, and he realized that if you had lost a wife, sweetheart, relations, a home or a livelihood it took some settling down with those who'd caused it.

Frank reckoned that if his drive

came up against such feelings, a Yankee might be able to handle them better than his own men. They saw his point but it still gnawed at them to have to take orders from a Yankee instead of from Johnny.

So the Hash Knife waited. Everything was ready for the drive; the cattle were in good shape, the remuda was complete, the chuck wagon was loaded, except for a few last minute items, and every man had seen to his own personal belongings. All they wanted now was for their curiosity to be satisfied.

It very soon would be. But the boss hadn't mentioned three men. Maybe this wasn't Cap Millet riding in. Nobody had said he was bringing two side-kicks. Yet somehow all the men knew they were watching Cap Millet.

Johnny sensed the resentment, tinged with curiosity, change to tension, spiced with hostility.

He knew that strangers didn't generally have this effect on the Hash Knife outfit. They were a pretty good crew, with peculiarities, naturally, but they were fairly tolerant with strangers while they weighed them up, then they were either downright friendly or just cussed hostile. They had had no time to size a man up on this occasion but Johnny knew they were hostile, but these were special circumstances.

Johnny got slowly to his feet. Around him some men fidgeted unknowingly, toying with a buckle, rubbing the butt of a Colt cradled in its holster or chewing imaginary tobacco. Some were just still, but whatever, every eye was on those three riders and Johnny would have bet that at that moment they saw only one — the man in the middle whose horse nosed that odd foot in front of the others. It was as if the other two riders held back slightly, giving him that mark of respect which set him aside.

The Hash Knife watched critically. They knew horses and set great store on how a man rode. This one rode easily, with an automatic adjustment to the movement of the animal, unthinkingly easing his weight, lightening the burden, an attitude born of a long time around horses. This man loved and respected them. He went up in the watchers' estimation but they still resented his coming.

Johnny kept his eyes on the lead rider, as he drew nearer, Johnny saw he was tall and lean like himself but there the comparison ended. There was a gaunt look about the stranger's face with the cheek-bones standing out. Trouble had left its mark. He was not particularly broad shouldered and Johnny got the impression that he was hunched in an effort to keep himself to himself. But he was not hunched and in his leanness there was a power, a power held back like a coiled spring ready to be unleashed. His face was burned brown from the lined forehead to the firm, clean-shaven, square chin.

Although he appeared to be taking no notice of his surroundings, Johnny realized differently when he focused on the stranger's eyes. They were alert, moving, seeing everything from beneath the battered brim of his stained Stetson. Johnny knew that they must have viewed each Hash Knife man in turn. But there was more to this man's eyes; there was a sadness. It raised a sympathy in Johnny for he figured that this man had suffered more than most.

Johnny glanced briefly at the other two riders and, as his eyes touched the one on the left, he sensed Clint Forbes, who was standing next to him, stiffen suddenly. He felt the tension in Clint reach explosive point and knew that Clint too had seen this man.

"A bloody nigger!" The words hissed snake-like from Clint's tight lips. There was venom and hatred in his voice. "We ain't havin' a bloody nigger on this drive."

Johnny sensed the mounting animosity in the others. "Ease up, boys," he drawled quietly but firmly. "Play it cool."

"But a bloody nigger!" protested Clint.

"I said ease it, Clint!" rapped Johnny in a tone which demanded obedience, and all knew that to step out of line would bring dire consequences from their foreman. "Let the boss handle it. I'll tell him they're here."

Johnny hurried to the veranda of the long, low ranch-house, stepped on to the wood and went into the house. A few moments later Frank Peters appeared with Johnny.

His square-shaped head, with dark hair greying at the temples, was set on a short, thick neck, which gave this broad, stocky man a look of extra strength. His sharp eyes were now clouded with anger which showed in the grim line of his lips, and the whiteness of his knuckles as he gripped the veranda rail tightly, trying to control his temper.

"I hired him, not two side-kicks as well, and certainly not a damned nigger!" Frank's voice rattled his annoyance.

Johnny said nothing but took in the two riders flanking the hunched horseman.

The negro was big. His strength could be seen in his muscles, which stood out against the tight shirt, and in the broad, deep chest which defied the top buttons to fasten. His face was expressionless and his big round eyes appeared to stare straight ahead, but Johnny knew better, for he had seen those eyes flicking over everyone. The whole of the Hash Knife had been noted in one flashing glance.

The white man was of medium height but broad and stocky with an air of toughness. He ran a fore finger under the battered brim of his Stetson, pushing it back from his forehead as if to give himself a better view. This movement revealed a rugged, angular, wind-burnt face. The lines around the corner of his eyes and mouth gave a pleasantness to his face which did not match his eyes. They smouldered with a serious concern for life and a distrust of everyone and everything until they were proved otherwise.

Although their horses were fresh, all three men bore the signs of long travel, and Johnny figured that, although they had come only twenty miles from town, they must have ridden far before yesterday.

The three riders reached the house and, still in their formation, turned their horses to face the veranda in front of Frank Peters.

Johnny was interested to see how his boss handled the situation. He was a hard man but fair and just. He paid the wages so he wanted a day's work for a day's pay, no more, no less. He had no time for slackers just as he couldn't abide crawlers. He was a good boss as long as you did right by him, which Johnny figured was fair enough. He'd stand up for his men if they were in the right but come down hard on them if they were in the wrong. They all knew exactly where they stood with him and, through his attitude had formed a good outfit. He realised exactly how they were feeling at this moment but he knew Cap and had hired him to do a job. Johnny found the situation intriguing.

Frank had strong definite views, that was why he had volunteered for the Confederate Army, but he was a tolerant man, he could understand other people's opinions and so bore no bitterness after the war. He accepted defeat as something which could not be altered. He realized it meant things would change so he just set about starting his life again, trying to rebuild the Hash Knife which had been started by his father. He knew the bitterness of defeat remained with some of his men but, so long as their attitudes didn't interfere with their work, he respected their feelings.

As he faced Cap Millet he knew how those men were feeling at the sight of a negro riding freely with a white man on to a Texas ranch.

"Cap," Frank nodded.

"Frank."

The greetings were over. Cap Millet had arrived.

"Come inside." Frank spoke directly at Cap. He swung round and strode for the door, calling over his shoulder, "You too, Johnny."

Cap swung from his horse in a smooth flowing action. He took the four steps on to the veranda in two strides and crossed the woodwork to follow Frank into the house. Johnny closed the front door behind him, and, as he went into the room on the right, his boss swung round on Cap.

"Why the hell have you brought that damned nigger with you?" Frank's eyes blazed with fury and his voice had a viciousness that comes with anger roused by the unexpected. Even Johnny was surprised by his boss's tone and attitude and he knew it had stung Cap for he sensed the Yankee stiffen.

Cap's eyes smouldered. "Nigger? You know better than to use that word, Frank." There was criticism and reprimand in the quiet but firm, forceful voice.

"Yes, I do," rapped Frank irritably, "but some of my men out there don't."

"Then you shouldn't hire them."

"Come off it, Cap." Frank showed his disgust with Cap's statement. "Losing a war doesn't change your opinions just like that. I want men who can do a job. My men can. That's all I'm interested in. Their beliefs have nothing to do with me so long as they don't interfere with the running of the Hash Knife, and I figure you're pushing those beliefs a bit hard right now."

"Then you get out there and tell them to tuck a bit of tolerance under their belts."

Frank bristled under what he considered amounted to an order. "You get rid of that black!" he countered.

Cap pursed his lips and looked thoughtfully at the toe of his right boot. He began to shake his head slowly, then he glanced up at Frank. "No!" he said firmly.

14

Frank's eyes narrowed. "I hired you, no sidekicks."

"Sure," agreed Cap, "but if I'm bossing a herd I do it my way, so I hired two more men."

"But you're asking for trouble."

"No, I'm not, nor is Josh. If there's trouble it'll be your boys who start it."

"I can't guarantee they won't, and you know it. I'm not their keeper. The best way to avoid trouble is to ride without Josh. So ease him out. You're hired for this one drive only. Josh can rejoin you at the end."

"No! We fought a war over this. Josh rides with me or you don't get me."

Frank's lips tightened grimly. Johnny could see he was having a hard time holding himself in check and Johnny was beginning to wonder why the boss didn't forget Cap altogether. Frank glanced at Johnny. "What's the feeling out there?"

"Explosive."

"Then why didn't it erupt when we rode in?" Cap figured that his question

15

would show that the two Hash Knife men were over-reading the situation.

"Because I've a damned good foreman who has the respect of the whole outfit. He's kept them in check."

Cap glanced at Johnny and nodded his approval. Johnny knew how the new man had summed him up.

Frank looked hard at Cap. "Let me tell you one thing, Johnny was taking this drive until I met you yesterday."

"Maybe you should have left it that way," said Cap. He glanced at Johnny again. "Surprised you're still here. Don't think I would have been if I'd had a job pulled from under me."

Johnny gave a half smile. "I figured you might need me, I reckon that's more so now." Before Cap could comment Johnny went on quickly. "Mr Peters is a good boss, what he says goes; it's good enough for me, besides the Hash Knife means something to me."

"Johnny and I came together after the war, he helped me build up the ranch again and I guess its got into his blood,"

Frank explained. "A job you could have done if you'd come back."

Johnny was startled by Frank's statement and Cap saw the puzzled look on the foreman's face.

"Yes, Johnny, I used to work for Frank before the war. Saw the trouble coming so I left about a year before hostilities broke out; reckoned coming from the north that my place was there."

Johnny nodded. "Coming for your old job back when Mr Peters met you yesterday?" A slight hostility had crept into Johnny's voice.

Cap smiled. "No. Just chance that I met Frank in town. I wasn't coming near the Hash Knife. No, Johnny, nobody's going to push you out. Frank asked my opinion on the situation up north. I told him and he figured a Northerner might just be better at handling any opposition you might meet up there. And I had experience last year on part of Chisholm's Trail. I reckoned I maybe owed Frank something for the years here, so I agreed." Cap eyed Johnny. "What's your attitude to working with a negro?"

"Any man can ride with me so long as he pulls his weight and bites on as much dust," replied Johnny. "But that don't go for all of them out there."

"Get rid of him, Cap, and have a peaceful ride," said Frank. "Why so keen on having him along? Why you riding with a negro?"

Cap looked hard at Frank. He hesitated, as if weighing up exactly what he should say or whether he should walk out and forget the drive, the Hash Knife and this whole goddamned business. But Cap had his principles. He had said he would take the Hash Knife cattle north for his old boss and that he meant to do. Any trouble would not be of his making.

"I told you yesterday that I got married two months after leaving the Hash Knife. What I didn't tell you was that Kathy was a Southerner."

"What!" Frank's surprised exclamation

told Johnny that there was a lot more behind Cap's statement.

"On my way north I took a job breaking in some horses for her father. Kathy and I fell in love at first sight. It was just there, Frank, we both sensed it. Something flowed between us right from that first meeting. We realized there could be trouble; I was heading north to a land which was fast approaching conflict with the South and Kathy's father was South through and through. I happened along when he was desperate for someone to break those horses or I wouldn't have got the job. Well, there's no need to tell you his attitude when his daughter said she was going to marry a goddamned Yankee. He tried all ways he could to stop her but Kathy was a match for him and she rode north with me. The only concession her father made was to give her one of his slaves — Josh."

Johnny glanced at his boss as Cap paused and he saw an understanding in his eyes. Frank nodded slowly but did not speak for he sensed in the pause Cap's desire to tell more. Johnny looked back at the new trail boss. He saw the sadness in Cap's eyes had heightened and he realized that Cap's recollection of his wife had put it there.

"I got a small spread, things were taking shape, we were happy, deeply so, thought the war when it came might pass us by. We put our heads in the sand, love blinded us, I suppose. We could see nothing else. I should have taken her further north, west, anywhere but where we stayed, but that place was there and it was beautiful. The war swamped us, passed right through after I'd gone."

"Kathy was there on her own?" queried Frank.

Cap tightened his lips, summoning his powers to carry on, for he had been hurt deep by the recollection, but he knew he must continue in order to explain Josh's presence outside, bringing tension to a cattle drive before it started.

"Josh worked for us and then I needed someone else so I hired Wade, who's out there now. Wade and I left at the same time to join the Army. I wanted Kathy to leave but she wouldn't, said she'd have Josh around and it would be better to keep to our own place — at that time it looked as if the war would never get near. I saw her twice in the next three years." Cap's voice faltered. Four years may have passed since the end of the war but Johnny knew that the past was coming back to Cap as vividly as if it was yesterday.

"The Confederates overran the area as they pushed north. Kathy as a Southerner figured she'd be all right if she stayed. She wasn't sure about Josh so he hid out in the woods. Everything was fine until you rebs were driven back. There was chaos in the retreat, stragglers everywhere, sometimes our patrols were in advance of them. Then I figure, defeat stuck in your throats and some of you bastards wreaked revenge on a Southerner who'd married a Yankee." Cap's eyes had narrowed with hate and anger and his voice spat out the words viciously. The room filled with tension, as Frank and Johnny waited for Cap to continue. "I was close to your rear, near enough home to slip away to see Kathy. I hadn't seen her for a year. God, how I wanted to feel her warmth, her softness, feel her hair, look into those deep blue eyes and hear her say my name. Just for her to be there, to drive away the horrors that were all about me and bring some sanity back, even for a few moments, to a mind warped by a bloody carnage I'd never wanted to be part of. I was concerned, worried for Kathy but somehow I imagined that the war would not touch her, but I hadn't reckoned on how it can turn honest, respectable human beings into vile, bestial devils."

Cap licked his lips. His eyes stared into the past. "I rode down the hill towards the house. It was raining hard, just as it had been for the past five days. There was mud everywhere. For a moment the years of horror passed away. I could have been riding home at the end of the day to the arms of a young, beautiful wife, to the warmth of a fire and food she had ready for me. Instead the house was cold and silent through the streaming rain and, as I leaned from the saddle to open the gate, I sensed something was wrong. It was then that I saw it, a crude cross at one end of a small mound of earth. It could have been anyone, but it was inside our broken fence. I knew it was Kathy. But I went through the motions, searching the house and shouting her name, but all I got was the howling wind, rattling shutters, banging doors and pounding rain.

"I came out of the house. There were the barn and stables but I knew it was useless to look there Kathy was lying in the rain-sodden ground. I turned, and a frightened Josh came reluctantly from the stable. Eventually I got him calmed down and reassured him that no more Johnny Rebs would come along. Then he managed to tell me what he knew. He'd come out of the woods two days previously, driven out by the sheer, cussed persistence of the rain. There were still rebs about so he was careful when he got near the buildings. He saw Kathy at one of the windows, then four rebs came down the roadway, half running, half sliding in the mud, dishevelled, scarred, bloody, the tattered remnants of a defeated army. They saw the house and went there. Josh heard them inside and half an hour later saw them come out carrying a body he recognized as Kathy. They scratched a shallow grave in the mud and were filling it in when a reb officer came up. A few words were exchanged and, when the grave was filled in, the officer said a few words in brief prayer and they left."

Cap, whose eyes had seen nothing during the telling, focused them on Frank. "They killed her, Frank, they

24

killed her. Four bloody rebs. I'm hunting them, Frank, and I'm going to kill every last bastard of them. Now you know why I ride with Josh, now you know why I take him with me wherever I go, why I take him on this drive. He knows them, Frank, the only man who does!"

Cap suddenly seemed to deflate, all his energy gone in the vivid remembering, in seeing it all again. Johnny felt a deep sympathy for him and he knew now why Cap wore that look of suffering. There was no telling how he had tortured himself imagining the horror of his wife's end.

Frank stirred from the intensity of his listening. "All right, Josh goes on the drive." He glanced at Johnny. "You keep the men in line."

"Right, boss."

Frank turned to Cap. "Why didn't you tell me this yesterday when I met you? I'd have understood. Just to tell me that you were looking for four men who had killed your wife — well, apart

25

from needing your help on the drive I figured bossing a trail drive might just make you forget revenge, but after hearing your story I know it's too deep so if you want to pull out of this job you can."

"Thanks, Frank, but I'll stick to my bargain, this drive is important to you."

"Good," said Frank. "Tell me one thing; the war's been over four years, how do you hope to find these men?"

"It's been a long search. I eventually tracked down their likely regiment, got the names of survivors and after speaking to a lot of them I narrowed it down. I got a break after talking to you yesterday. I was enquiring about the officer who was at the grave and learned he's two days ride from here." Cap looked at Johnny. "Can you handle the drive for four days?"

"Sure.

"Then point 'em north and I'll join you along the trail."

"You said I. What about Josh and Wade?"

26

"They can ride with Johnny, it'll give your outfit a chance to get used to them."

"But won't you need Josh to identify the man?"

"No. He's not going to deny he was there. He had nothing to do with and presumably knows nothing about the killing."

# 2

WHEN Johnny stepped into the glare of the Texas sun he felt an atmosphere to match its heat. His eyes swept the scene in one penetrating glance. Josh and Wade had dismounted, and Johnny realized that, sensing hostility, they had casually positioned themselves so that every Hash Knife man was covered should the antagonism erupt into the open. The Hash Knife hands were edgy, even those who Johnny knew were not anti-negro, but they were putting their loyalty to the men with whom they rode first.

Johnny's lips tightened. He knew he had to get the situation under control immediately or the start of the drive could be jeopardised.

He stopped at the top of the veranda steps. "All right. Hear this." The sharpness of his voice cut through the hostility. It demanded attention, important things, concerning them all, were going to be said; they had to listen. "The drive starts immediately." Get the men occupied, keep them that way give them something to think about. "Charlie, finish loading the chuck-wagon, Red, give him a hand. Josh, you good with horses?" Bring in Cap's men, don't isolate them, make everyone feel they have an equal share of taking the herd north.

"Sure thing," replied Josh.

"Figured you might be," said Johnny. "Take charge of the remuda."

Josh was now thrown in with everyone. He had a responsibility to each man. He had to look after one hundred and two horses, ten for each man and two extra for the trail-drive boss, see they were fit, have a particular one ready when its rider called for it, so he had to be familiar with the animals quickly and speedy with his identification. Because of the nature of his job each man was thrown into close contact with the negro. Johnny knew he was running the risk of abrasive attitudes creating explosive situations but he figured that the dependence of the whites on the negro and the responsibility of the negro to the whites could bring about a closer harmony, breaking down man-made barriers, leading to a harmonious crew for a drive which could test all their relationships.

"Clint, you ride segundo to me until Cap joins us."

This announcement surprised the Hash Knife cowboys. So the stranger wasn't riding with them right away. Johnny was bossing them. Well, that suited. But Johnny's choice of second in command was curious. It put Clint in a position of authority with jurisdiction over the negro and Clint was a negro hater, but they figured Johnny knew what he was doing. Maybe he reckoned Clint's added responsibility would keep him fully occupied, and Johnny could come down on him heavy if he let any trouble develop from anyone with a dislike of negroes.

"The rest of you keep tag on the beeves. We work as one team, all taking turns to chew dust at drag; no one gets any favours. This drive's important for the Hash Knife's survival and so to your jobs, so let's have no trouble." Johnny paused to let his words sink in. There wasn't a man there who didn't know to what he was referring. He glanced round his crew and saw no queries. "All right, we'll make our choices from the remuda." He looked at Wade. "Guess you know what your boss likes so you can make first choice for him."

The men followed Johnny to the remuda which was corralled a short distance from the ranch-house. As the cowboys gathered along one side of the corral, Wade cast his eye over the horses and then, with a selection made, cut out twelve he thought would suit Cap. The Hash Knife hands watched him critically. They saw a competent, workmanlike display. They admired his efficiency but they saw nothing to enthuse over.

Johnny took his turn, cut out ten horses for himself and Clint followed suit. Johnny supervised the drawing of lots which decided the order in which the rest of the outfit should cut out one horse at a time until they had the required ten.

Throughout the whole procedure Josh was alert, noting identifying marks, memorising and linking them with the man who had cut them out. It was no easy matter but Josh figured he had just about got them tagged by the time the selection was over. He was determined not to slip up, he didn't want to give the Hash Knife boys the slightest chance to ignite the antagonism towards him, which he had sensed when he arrived at the Hash Knife.

Johnny allocated the men to their positions for the start of the drive and each one chose the horse he was going to use first, threw a Texas saddle on its back, and left the rest of the remuda to Josh.

Johnny rode over to the ranch-house and met Frank Peters and Cap Millet as they came outside.

"We're all set, Mr Peters," Johnny reported.

"Good." Frank glanced at Cap. "Any instructions?"

"No. Just keep 'em moving north, Johnny."

"Right." Johnny looked at his boss. "Don't worry Mr Peters, we'll get them there."

Frank smiled. "Good luck."

Johnny turned his horse and rode over to the men who were mounted and waiting for him. The chuck-wagon, drawn by four mules, had left ten minutes ago to get ahead of the herd and be ready at the night rendezvous, which Johnny would choose later in the afternoon before the herd got there.

"Let's ride!" Johnny called.

The men turned their mounts to follow, while Josh cut away to the remuda and set it into a walking pace to the left of the trail which the cattle would take.

The riders found the herd of two thousand five hundred cattle grazing contentedly a mile from the ranch-house, watched over by three Hash Knife hands who were staying behind. The cattle were in good condition, carefully chosen, strength being an important consideration for the long drive. The pale-coloured long-legged longhorns began to move slowly as they were pressed by the riders taking up their positions. Johnny rode quickly, seeming to be everywhere, supervising the start of the trail drive.

Clint Forbes, Fox Honeyman and Jim Lovell ranged themselves along the left side of the herd while Wade Lawson, Rod Forrest and Joe Durham positioned themselves on the opposite side, leaving Red Fletcher and Barney McNeil to ride drag.

As they galloped to the back of the herd Red and Barney pulled their bandanas over their faces to combat the choking dust rising behind the herd as it headed away from the Hash Knife.

With the lead cattle sorted out Clint Forbes and Joe Durham, riding point, headed them in the required direction before settling to their positions out and back from the leaders. From here the two men, by riding forward and closing in as required, were able to control the direction of the herd which was soon strung out in a long column like some slow, advancing army.

Fox Honeyman and Wade Lawson, at swing, rode well out from the herd preventing any cattle from straying, while Jim Lovell and Rod Forrest took up flank positions.

The riders eased the pressure once the cattle settled to steady forward movement, but they kept a vigilant restraint on them though the animals were not allowed to know it. Skill and expertise gentled the longhorns on their way yet allowed them a sense of freedom which kept them calm and quiet.

Johnny was pleased with the way the herd quickly settled to a steady pace which, without mishap, would enable them to cover about twenty miles a day. He swung wide behind the herd, keeping out of the swirling dust, which rose from the hooves and choked at the drag men, who whipped in the strays and pressed any loiterers. Johnny urged his horse alongside the flank of moaning longhorns and sought out Clint.

"Going to scout out a bed ground," Johnny called. "They're moving well, keep it that way."

Clint raised his hand in acknowledgement. Satisfied with the behaviour of the lead steers, Clint relaxed in the saddle, closed his ears to the bellows and moans of the longhorns and watched Johnny ride ahead of the herd. His lips set in a grim line as he wondered who his foreman would back if ever a showdown came over Josh.

Johnny caught up with the chuck-wagon about three miles ahead of the herd, had a brief word with Charlie and rode on. After eight miles Johnny found the bedding ground he was looking for, an area of dry, matted grass of the previous summer's growth, slightly elevated above the rest of the range so it would catch any breeze, which had been lacking on the lower ground all day. Under these conditions the cattle should bed easily and, granted any unforeseen happenings, should spend a peaceful night.

On his way back Johnny informed Charlie where he would bed the herd. The cook quickened his mules' pace so that he could be settled, with a meal ready, by the time the rest of the outfit rode in.

Sighting the herd, Johnny was pleased it was still making good progress. Once he had his report from Clint, he informed his segundo that, because of the ideal situation of the bedding ground, he had decided to cut short the day's travel and use it.

Once they reached the night stop, the herd settled quickly and, when the riders came in for supper, Johnny allocated the rota of night guards for the drive.

The sky was clear, the gentle breeze, which started to stir the grass as darkness swept across the Texas plains, was soft and some of the heat of the day spilled over into the mildness of the night. Johnny was satisfied with the way things had gone on the first day of the drive. There had been no trouble, the riders had settled into their work well and there was no apparent animosity to the two new men. But, as he rolled himself in his blankets, Johnny suffered no illusions about the attitude of some of the men to Josh. Their hatred had not disappeared because they had started on the long drive north; it was still there and Johnny knew it would not take much to bring it exploding into the open. But he'd be content if he got over the first few days, until Cap arrived, without any trouble. Not that he would be relieved of all responsibility then, for, as Cap's segundo and as foreman of the Hash Knife, Cap would expect him to keep the men in check.

Throughout the next three days the herd moved steadily northwards. Johnny was satisfied, he could have pushed harder to gain a few more miles but, at the pace they maintained, the cattle gave little trouble and the men, though always vigilant, were able to relax some and not over-stretch themselves, horses were conserved and, all in all, the first trail drive for the Hash Knife was going well.

Johnny pulled his jacket tighter around him against the sharpening chill in the wind as he rode to check with the night riders circling the herd. The men he had left in camp laid out their bedrolls closer to the fire.

The wind disturbed the horses and some showed a tendency to stray, so Josh hobbled the worst offenders. He found little space when he brought his bed-roll to the fire but he squeezed between two unoccupied bed-rolls.

As he squatted and unrolled his blankets he sensed every man's eyes on him. What the hell was wrong? Why should these Southern bastards stare? Goddamned Texans. He hadn't wanted to ride with them but Cap had taken this job so he rode. The sooner he was out of these Southern States the better. He wanted no trouble so he'd go on eating humble pie unless these cursed Southerners went too far. He had as much right to warmth as they had.

Appearing unconcerned he continued to prepare his bed. He felt the tension heighten. He stiffened and stopped his bed-making when two spurred boots stepped into his vision. He waited for them to move, but knew they would not. Only one man in the Hash Knife outfit wore such fancy spurs — Clint Forbes! Josh stared at the boots, then slowly his large eyes moved up, scanned the trousers, crossed the shirt to the face which glared down at him.

A contemptuous smile touched the corners of Clint's mouth. The hate in his eyes was laced with pleasure derived from the knowledge that the situation was going to develop to his satisfaction.

Their eyes met and held each other. Josh saw Clint's innermost feelings, his loathing for the blacks and for those who were not white. His hatred of anyone coloured was directed at Josh, he was to be the whipping boy, he could pay for all the coloured people in the world.

Clint wondered why Cap rode with a good-for-nothing black. Why put himself on the level of a nigger? Well, he'd show this black bastard a thing or two; he'd put him in his place.

"You ain't sleeping there!" The words lashed from Clint's tight lips.

"There's nowhere else." Josh's words were quiet but firm.

"There's plenty of room out there." Clint nodded in the direction of the prairie beyond their immediate circle.

"It's cold."

"That's too bad, but you ain't sleeping next to me, so git."

Josh glanced at the men around the fire. The flames lit up the hatred in most eyes and an eagerness to have done with this nigger who dared to ride with them. Where he saw sympathy he also saw inaction. Those men would not go against their own, they put loyalty to the Hash Knife first. He looked at Wade. Wouldn't he speak up for him? Or was it a case of too many whites so side with them by doing nothing?

"Nor next to me." Joe Durham stood behind him on the other empty bed-roll.

"Git to hell out of here!" Clint's voice carried a viciousness, forecasting physical hurt if Josh ignored him.

He hesitated only a fraction of a second longer then, knowing his position was hopeless, he started to roll up his bedding.

The tension relaxed a little as a ripple

of laughter flowed round the group, confirming their approval of Clint's victory.

"Hold it!" Heads turned to find the speaker was Wade Lawson. "He has the same right as you to be near the fire."

The tension was back.

"Like hell he has!" There was anger in Clint at this interference. "And you keep you bloody nose out of this, Lawson."

"He has a right . . . "

"He's no right," Joe Durham boomed. Wade's hand lowered near the butt of his Colt. Joe noticed it. "Go for it, Lawson, it'll give me the greatest pleasure to blow you to hell. You damned Yankees killed two of my brothers because of the likes of this trash. So let him go and save a lot of trouble."

"Cool it, Wade," said Josh. "Don't get into trouble over me. I'll sleep out there." Josh grasped his bedroll then straightened to his full height. His eyes locked on Clint for a brief moment then he passed and moved away from the brightness of the fire.

Wade seethed. His eyes flashed round the faces, lit by the dancing flames, but he saw no help, and Joe Durham was still daring him to draw. His lips tightened and, with anger boiling inside, he stooped down, swept his bedding into his arms, lifted his saddle and hurried after Josh. He felt the tension behind him ease, sensed the delight the Hash Knife were feeling in their victory and heard the snide remark of "nigger lover" thrown after him.

Wade reached Josh just as he dropped his blankets on the spot he had chosen to spend the night. "You should have stayed near the warmth, Wade," said Josh as the white man put his belongings on the ground.

"Bloody bastards!" commented Wade viciously. "Ain't they heard we won the war?"

Josh smiled. "Winning a war don't change attitudes overnight. It'll take a long time, longer than us, for the hatred to work out."

"Let them settle down then I figure we sneak in, take that son-of-a-bitch, Clint, and teach him a lesson."

"Cool it, Wade," replied Josh calmly, trying to ease the anger which was close to snapping point. "Sure, I'd like to fix him but now ain't the time, it'll only lead to more trouble."

"But . . . " started Wade.

"No," cut in Josh. "Leave it. Mister Cap will be back soon; we'll see if those no good cowpokes will buck me then. Come on, get some sleep." Josh laid down on his blanket and pulled another round him, putting a finish to Wade's suggestion.

Two hours later Johnny rode in, unsaddled his horse and made for the circle of fire-light. It would be good to feel some warmth and drive out the chill which had crept in with the night. Johnny hoped it wasn't the portent of bad weather. Things were going nicely; he didn't want the herd spooking by a storm. The foreman stopped sharply. Two blanketed forms lay a few strides away.

"What the . . . ?" This was no night for men to be sleeping this far from the fire. Johnny's thoughts puzzled for a reason. He moved close. Josh! Johnny guessed the other to be Wade. There must have been trouble! Johnny was annoyed. He did not consider the sleeping men. A sharp kick at their feet brought them awake and sitting up instantly.

"Why the hell are you sleeping out here?" he demanded roughly.

"We wanted to," replied Josh.

"Like hell you did." Johnny's tone was curt. He wanted no nonsense. He wanted the truth.

The two men scrambled to their feet and faced his anger.

"We were bedding down for the night but Clint wouldn't have Josh sleep next to him and there was no more room near the fire." Wade offered an explanation.

Johnny's lips tightened. Damn Clint. "Get your things," he ordered.

"Leave it, Mister Johnny, don't cause trouble," said Josh.

"I'm bossing this outfit, now get your things."

The two men did as they were told and followed their boss to the sleeping forms around the fire. Johnny dropped his things within the circle of light, bent down and picked up two tin mugs lying close to the glowing wood.

"On your feet!" The silence was suddenly shattered by his shout and by the crash of tin against tin as he banged the mugs together. He went round the circle of sleepers continuing to shout and kicking their feet. In a few moments the whole outfit was facing their boss and muttering curses, under their breath, at this unceremonious awakening.

Johnny glared at them all, the firelight picking out the anger in his eyes. "Josh sleeps here!" the words were simple but decisive. They formed an order presented in a way which would tolerate no dissent. He eyed Clint. "And you as segundo should have seen that he did."

"Boss, he's a nigger," protested Clint.

"He sweats under the sun like you, he chews dust like you, he's here to see the herd safely to its destination like you are, so I figure he's entitled to warmth like you are." Johnny's anger was so evident that none of the Hash Knife protested any further. They knew Johnny and knew that in this mood he was not to be contradicted. "Josh is in charge of the remuda, your mounts, if they aren't fit and ready when you want them then you'll find yourselves on foot and a man on foot ain't a herd rider; he's useless. Josh has an important job and I want him fit for that job and it ain't helping to push him out there to sleep." Johnny paused, waiting for any dissension but none came. "All right, spread out and make room for three more."

The men shuffled away to move their

bedding; only Clint hesitated but when he met Johnny's eyes he moved.

The following morning Johnny took Clint to one side. "I know your feelings for blacks but just rein them in. We want this herd safely to Kansas. It ain't going to be easy, so let's have no trouble of our making. As segundo you're here to stop trouble not to cause it."

"I won't be segundo for much longer." Clint's voice was cold. He swung on his heel before Johnny could speak and hurried to his horse.

Johnny watched him go, choosing to ignore the undercurrent of threat in Clint's words.

# 3

CAP MILLET halted his horse at the top of the rise. He eased his Stetson and wiped his forehead. The Texas sun had blazed unmercifully for two days and Cap was glad the ride was almost over.

Before him the two-mile slope levelled at the small town of Durango. Beyond, a gentle valley, bordered on each side by low, rounded hills, stretched into the blue haze of distance. It looked a pleasant place, the sort he and Kathy might have chosen if she had lived and they had come back south.

The thought of his wife stirred him to the purpose of his visit to Durango. If he was right, the first real contact on his ride of revenge was down there.

Cap tapped his horse forward. The dust of the dry trail was disturbed only momentarily under the hooves as the chestnut was held to a walking pace. It was too hot to hurry even though Cap was anxious to be on. He had to consider his horse with at least two, possibly three, days riding to reach the herd.

No one moved in Durango; the heat was overpowering. Sheltered by hills on three sides, it attracted the heat, holding it to itself. Along the full length of Main Street only half a dozen men lounged in the shade of the sidewalk's awning. The sheriff and his deputy eyed the lone horseman from their chairs tipped back against the wall of their office.

"What fool rides at this part of the day?" muttered the deputy.

The sheriff made no comment but scrutinized the stranger carefully. He knew that the rider was alert, that he had the layout of the town quickly stored in his mind through his sharp eyes which swept the whole street from below the brim of his stained Stetson.

The sheriff was curious. This man must be here for a purpose; otherwise why ride in this god-damned heat and why be concerned with Durango? The sheriff ran a peaceful town nothing out of the ordinary ever happened. There was the usual spate of drunks on a Saturday night when cowboys from local ranches came for a night out. There was the odd quarrel to sort out but on the whole the folks of Durango and its neighbourhood gave little trouble.

He kept his eye on strangers, moved them on if they weren't looking to settle, and made sure they knew they were dealing with a lawman who wanted no trouble but who would deal with it effectively and quickly to Durango's benefit. The sheriff reckoned he was a judge of strangers but this one affected him differently. There was something about this rider which was — well the sheriff couldn't put his finger on it and it irritated him not to be able to do so.

He watched the stranger as he rode slowly past, eyed him as he turned his horse to the rail outside the saloon, admired the easy flow of his body as he dismounted and was surprised to see the stranger tall and erect, something which was belied by the way he had appeared hunched in the saddle.

Cap slapped dust from his shirt and pants, glanced at the sign, The Gilded Cage, climbed on to the sidewalk and pushed through the batwings.

The sheriff spoke briefly to his deputy, pushed himself to his feet, stretched and sauntered to the Gilded Cage. He paused at the batwings to look over the curved top into the long room. A dozen men, seeking shelter from the sun and solace for their thirst, were scattered at the tables while two leaned against the bar. The stranger stood at one end of the counter cupping his beer to his lips. The sheriff sent the batwings squeaking and strolled to the bar to stand a few feet from the newcomer.

"Beer," ordered the sheriff.

His eyes met those of the stranger through the mirror which stretched along the wall behind the counter.

"Checking me out, sheriff? Protecting your town?" Cap's voice was low but distinctive.

The sheriff saw a smile flick the stranger's lips and disappear. He stiffened; the stranger had read him.

"I do my duty. Passing through?"

"A brief call."

The sheriff's mind went back to his first impressions. They were no clearer now except that he had confirmation that this man was on a purposeful visit; he was no drifter. The sheriff felt uneasy but he still couldn't put his finger on the reason.

"How brief?" asked the lawman.

"Depends how long it takes me to locate someone." Cap eyed the sheriff through the mirror. He saw a man of medium build with a rugged face, angular jawed. The sheriff, whom he judged to be in his mid-forties, gave the impression that he was not a man to meddle with, a man whom it was better to ride with than against. Cap had no need to needle him and he aimed to keep it that way. "Maybe you can help me."

"Maybe. I know all the folks around."

"Steve Nolan mean anything to you?" Although Cap watched the lawman closely he gained nothing from the expression on his face.

"Who wants to know?"

"Cap Millet."

"That you?"

"I want to know, so that's me."

The sheriff looked thoughtfully. Now he knew why he had this strange feeling about this man. Millet's purpose in Durango did concern him.

"Well?" prompted Cap.

"Sure, I know Steve Nolan." The sheriff turned to face Cap without the mirror between. Cap met his gaze, waiting for him to continue. "What you want him for?"

"That's my business."

The sheriff's eyes narrowed. "And mine, if it's likely to upset the peace of my town."

Cap smiled. "You sure pamper this place. No, I ain't likely to trouble your goddamned town. Now tell me where I can find Nolan and I'll be on my way."

The sheriff drained his beer, eyed Cap then said "Come on." He turned from the counter and made for the batwings.

Surprised, Cap followed. Once outside the saloon the sheriff headed for his office. Cap caught him up and fell into step beside him.

"No need for a personal escort," Cap said. "Just tell me where he is."

The sheriff ignored Cap's comment. "You've ridden a long way to see Steve," he said, eyeing Cap's dust-covered horse. "And you don't intend to stay in Durango long. Now, that could indicate gunplay with you confident of coming out on top."

Cap laughed. "You sure are a suspicious cuss, but I can't say I blame you. There'll be no gunplay in Steve's case."

The sheriff stiffened. "What do you mean, in Steve's case? You figuring on gunning someone else?"

"Maybe, but I reckon it won't be around here."

The deputy watched the two men approach. He let his chair swing forward on its four legs and nodded when the two men stopped in front of him.

The sheriff kept his eyes on Cap. "Like you to meet my deputy, Steve Nolan!" Cap's surprise showed but the sheriff learned no more. He looked at his deputy. "Steve, this here's Cap Millet, come to Durango to see you." He saw his deputy was even more surprised than Millet and he figured Steve didn't know the stranger.

Steve eyed Cap with some suspicion. "Me? Sure you got the right fella?"

"You the Steve Nolan who served under General Price, a lieutenant?"

Steve nodded. "Sure."

"Then you're the right fella." Cap had surveyed the seated man as they spoke. He saw a man of twenty-four with no outward scars of war, but there was no telling how it had marred the youngster inside. His eyes were clear and bright with a hint of suspicion still in them as he met Cap's gaze firmly. Cap detected in the strong facial lines an utter loyalty to any friend and a tolerance of any man until something ran against him. Cap knew the sheriff had a good deputy in Steve Nolan.

"Cap Millet?" Steve toyed with the words thoughtfully. "Nope. Can't say I've heard of you, but if I judge rightly you served with the other side."

Cap smiled. "You're perceptive." He paused a moment as if picking his words. "I'd like you to think back to a time nearing the war's end."

"Don't like to think on those things," put in Steve with a frown. "That damned war's best forgotten."

"How right you are," agreed Cap, "but sometimes there are things you can't forget."

"Like what?"

Cap knew from Steve's look that the

horrors of the war had done their best to damage a young mind, but he realized that Steve was winning his battle to wipe out the memories. Cap was sorry for having to make him recall something from the carnage.

"Please bear with me, I'm really here to thank you," said Cap reassuringly.

"Thank me?"

"Towards dark one day you came to a house six miles out of Jettersville. There'd been incessant rain for days; it was still raining; there was mud everywhere."

"And bodies, and blood," added Steve between lips drawn tight in the grimness of recall.

"Near that house you saw four soldiers burying a woman." Cap's voice was cold, expressionless with hurt at remembering a happening which he had only been able to picture in his mind.

Steve stared at Cap. A scene, long forgotten, flashed vividly, recalled from the subconscious depths by Cap's words. An incident, insignificant to Steve, meant something to this man, whose eyes reflected a hidden sadness at its recall.

"Yes." Steve's one word carried with it a confirmation and a query as to why Millet should seek him out now to mention a small moment in time from so long ago.

"She was my wife." The words came quietly, scarcely above a whisper but the lawmen could not mistake them. Stunned, they stared at Cap without speaking. They had the answer to the sadness in his eyes. "A negro who worked for us, scared out of his wits by what had been happening during those days, saw four soldiers go into the house. They came out later carrying a body and proceeded with a burial. He saw you arrive and say a few words over the grave. I want to thank you for that."

"It was nothing," replied Steve. "Hadn't much time with Union troops so close. When I saw four Confederates, I wondered why they weren't getting to hell out of there instead of conducting a burial. When I asked them why they said . . . " Steve paused. He met Cap's eyes intent upon him and he knew this man wanted the truth no matter what it was. "They said they'd found her dead. Not a pretty sight, some sadistic bastard had used her . . . " Steve's voice faltered when he saw hurt and pain grip Cap. He glanced at the sheriff and he knew he too had seen what lay deep in Cap. "They said they couldn't leave her." Steve went on. "They regretted the rough, quick burial, but you know how it was. I said a few words and we left."

As Steve finished speaking Cap took a grip on himself. He breathed deeply and asked, "You didn't question them about it?"

"No. Why should I?" Steve was puzzled by Cap's query. "They'd given me an explanation. Besides there wasn't time. Would you have held an enquiry with Union troops breathing down your neck?"

"Guess not." Cap knew Steve was right. He couldn't blame him for not probing the incident. "You had no reason to doubt their story?"

"No." Steve looked curiously at Cap. "Say, what you getting at?" he asked, pushing himself from his chair.

"Rape! Murder! My wife was alive when those four soldiers arrived. The negro knew. He'd seen her at the window. Those men were in the house half an hour!" Cap's eyes flashed with need for the bloody revenge which had been tearing at his heart for four years.

"You've only a goddamned negro's word and imagination for it," said Steve harshly. "Those men said they were looking for food, found your wife dead and couldn't leave her as she was. I had no reason to doubt their word."

"Then you don't know that they didn't rape and murder."

Steve stared at Cap in disbelief as the sudden realization that something which he had never contemplated could be true.

"I suppose not," he said half reluctantly, "but I can be no more sure that they didn't than you can that they did."

"Damn it all, man, why should four soldiers want to bury a woman in the middle of a retreat with the enemy close unless they had something to hide?"

"You've sure convinced yourself that that's what happened and I guess you'll never rest until you've found out." There was a touch of pity in Steve's voice. "Well, I'm sorry I can't help you. As far as I know, and believe, those boys didn't do it. I guess if they had they'd have got to hell out of there mighty fast. As for burying something they wanted to hide — well you've a sound argument, but strange things happen in war. I saw hard-bitten soldiers moved to compassion in the strangest ways, and these four must have figured it was right to give your wife a burial rather than leave her."

Cap's anger had been soothed by Steve's tone. He realized that neither could prove the other wrong. He shrugged his shoulders. "Well, some day maybe I'll find the truth."

"You figure on finding the four soldiers?" The sheriff spoke for the first time. "This land's a mighty big place and the war's four years gone."

"I'll find them. It took me over three years to find their names and . . . "

"You know them?" Steve was amazed. He had hoped the matter was finished but now he knew Cap would confront him further.

"Yes." Cap kept his eyes on Steve, ready to seize on anything which showed that Steve knew more than he cared to admit. "Jess Sharp, Walt Mason, Pete Carter, Don White, and Rowdy Martin." He saw the quick, almost imperceptible exchange of glances between the lawmen and he knew that some or all the names meant something to them.

"You said there were four but you've named five," the sheriff pointed out.

"I'm not sure which four. I was

64

hoping Steve might be able to help me."

Steve's mind was pounding as the names hit him, recalling that grim scene so far away, four years ago. He knew them but should he admit it? Cap was going to hunt them down, was going to extract the truth. If there was truth in Cap's story, Steve wondered if he had the right to condemn them to a confrontation with a man bent on a deadly revenge. Or should he eliminate an innocent man?

"Come on, Steve, I can see you know. I'll find out sooner or later so you may as well tell me now," Cap urged.

Steve glanced at his sheriff and saw the older man nod.

"Don White wasn't one of them," he answered quietly.

"Thanks," said Cap. "Now do you know where any of them are?"

"Only one," replied Steve. "If I knew where any of the others were I wouldn't tell you. I believe they're innocent, but there's one I don't mind telling you about." Steve turned towards the door of the office. "Come on, I'll show you something."

The sheriff followed his deputy and Cap into the office. Steve stopped in front of a board to which several notices were pinned and pointed to one of them. "Wanted for Robbery, Rape and Murder, Pete Carter, alias Butch." The words hammered at Cap and one word pounded more than the others. The same word suddenly impressed the two lawmen who exchanged glances of surprised alarm. The notice had been on their board over a month; the exact wording had been forgotten; it had become just another Wanted poster to them.

Cap, fired with anger, swung on Steve. "There, that's all I need!" His finger rapped at the word on the poster. "Rape! Carter wanted for rape!"

"Steady, Millet," said the sheriff, "that's no proof they raped your wife."

"No, but it makes it more than likely. When did you last hear of Carter?"

"Fortnight ago. Fifty miles to the east," replied the sheriff. "We've been alerted, heard he'd moved nearer Durango, but nothing certain."

Cap scowled. Fifty miles east was going to take him further away from the herd, but he couldn't miss this chance. He figured Johnny could take care of the drive a little longer. "Thanks," he said to the two lawmen. "And thanks again, Steve, for those words over Kathy." He swung out of the office and started towards his horse tied to the rail outside the saloon. The two lawmen came on to the sidewalk but all three pulled up short when they saw a rider, tall in the saddle, dressed completely in black from his low-crowned sombrero to his high heeled riding boots.

"Wes Griffiths!" The sheriff whispered the name with some contempt. He disliked bounty hunters almost as much as the men they hunted. He knew Cap had recognized the man who rode the chestnut, leading a black across the back of which a body was slung face down.

Cap, wanting to be on his way, was held by the sight of the infamous bounty hunter, riding at a deliberate, walking pace along the centre of the street. Griffiths cut an impressive figure and, though Cap detested the trade the bounty hunter followed, he couldn't help but admire the impression the physical presence made.

Griffiths halted his horse in front of the three men. "Butch Carter." He indicated the body on the horse.

Cap stiffened but wasn't surprised. Something seemed to have told him that the rider he had seen, on coming out of the sheriff's office, was bringing Carter in.

The sheriff stepped down off the sidewalk and pulled the dead man's head upwards by the hair to make an identification. Satisfied, he let the head drop. "Take care of things, Steve. Come inside, Griffiths." The sheriff stepped on to the sidewalk and as he passed Cap he commented, "That saves you looking."

Griffiths who had swung out of the saddle and was following the sheriff, with a smile flicking the corner of his lips, glanced at Cap. "Sorry, I beat you to the reward."

Cap eyed Griffiths coldly. "I ain't a bounty hunter. Just wanted to talk to him."

"Guess you're too late," smiled Griffiths and passed on into the office.

Steve lifted the body from the horse and laid it on the sidewalk. He sent someone from the small knot of people, who had started to gather, to get the undertaker. He emptied the dead man's pockets and saddle bags.

A piece of paper attracted his attention. He unfolded it and glanced quickly at the writing. He looked up at Cap whose hate-filled eyes were staring at the dead man.

He had lost the opportunity of physical revenge on someone he was certain had raped and murdered his wife, but his mind was taking that revenge now. Steve felt some sympathy

69

for Cap when he saw how the need for revenge had gnawed so deep, leaving an ugly scar which was reflected in Cap's eyes as he stared at the body.

Steve held out the piece of paper. "Here, I guess you'd like to see this."

The words broke sharply into Cap's vengeance. He started and saw the paper in Steve's outstretched hand. He took it and read. The message meant nothing to him except to indicate that the writer was in the army, but the signature sent his mind grasping at another lead. Jess Sharp! He glanced at the top of the page. Two scrawled words stood out. Fort Worth! Jess Sharp had written this from Fort Worth!

Cap was hardly able to grasp his luck. His ride to Durango had been well worthwhile. He handed the paper back to Steve. "Thanks," he said and the lawman saw the appreciation in Cap's eyes.

Cap turned and hurried to his horse. Steve straightened and watched him. He admired the easy swing into the saddle and the gentle persuasion of the hands on the reins.

The sheriff followed Wes Griffiths from the office and joined his deputy as the bounty hunter strolled to the saloon.

The two lawmen watched Cap ride out of town.

"I sure hope he finds the truth," said Steve quietly.

# 4

IT was mid-afternoon when Johnny, riding ahead of the herd, saw a lone rider break the skyline of the rise two miles to the east. The horseman set his mount in the direction of the herd and it was not long before Johnny recognized the seemingly hunched style of Cap Millet. Johnny turned his horse to meet him.

They exchanged curt greetings and, as Johnny turned his horse alongside Cap, he saw that there still remained the preoccupied sadness of a man set on revenge, of a man who would know no peace until he knew the truth and had avenged his wife's murder. Johnny wondered about Cap's visit to Durango but he asked no questions and got no answers.

"How's the drive?" asked Cap.

"Fine, everything going smoothly."

"No trouble?" Cap put the question as if he figured Johnny was hiding something.

"Nothing that wasn't easily settled."

"Tell me," pressed Cap when Johnny offered no explanation. "I want right in on the situation."

Johnny told his story.

"Clint Forbes a trouble maker?" queried Cap.

"No, normally a fairly easygoing man. Good worker, good rider, good with cattle and horses. But he just don't like blacks."

"Seems he respects your authority if he knuckled under without more protest."

"Respects the Hash Knife."

"Then let's hope he continues to see that any trouble could run against the Hash Knife." He looked over the herd critically. "Moving nicely," he commented.

Johnny had no time to reply as the flank rider wheeled his horse and rode towards them. Wade's pleasure at seeing

Cap was evident when they exchanged greetings.

"I'd like to have a word with Wade and Josh about my trip to Durango, mind if I take him?" Cap asked Johnny.

"Sure. I'll ride flank for him."

"Thanks. We shan't be long, then I'll ride with you to find a bed-ground."

Cap and Wade rode off in the direction of the remuda. Josh's teeth showed white against his blackness when his lips parted in a broad grin at the sight of Cap.

"Glad to see you back, Mister Cap," he called as he brought his horse to a halt in front of the two riders.

Cap nodded his greeting. "Heard you had some trouble."

"Mister Johnny straightened it out. There'll be no more now you're back," replied Josh.

"Don't bank on it. Hate can run deep in some men." Cap looked thoughtful. "Sometimes I wonder about myself," he muttered to himself.

"Did you find Steve Nolan?"

"Yes. He was deputy sheriff in Durango."

"Get any leads on the others?"

"Yes. Pete Carter was wanted for murder and rape so I reckon we're on to the right men."

"Was?" queried Wade.

"Yes. He's dead."

"You found him. You killed him?" Josh's eyes widened into whiteness.

"No. A bounty hunter brought him in while I was in Durango. There was letter in his pocket from Jess Sharp in the Army at Fort Worth."

"Right on our trail." Wade seized on the information.

Cap nodded. "Maybe another four days' drive if all goes well."

Cap slipped easily into command and, though the Hash Knife riders would have preferred Johnny to remain boss, they came quickly to respect Cap's skills and judgement, and they tolerated the fact that, in their eyes, he was still a Yankee.

But Joe Durham voiced his deep

dislike, stemming from the death of his brothers during the war. "Two bloody Yankees among us now," he complained to Clint.

"Sure. And that damned nigger's getting too cocky since Millet returned."

The Hash Knife cattle moved steadily north and four nights later, as Cap and Johnny were drawing their coffee from the pot on the fire, Cap said, "We'll halt them early tomorrow, should be close to Fort Worth, and give all the crew time for relaxation."

At the noon stop the next day Cap told the riders of his intention and issued a rota for minding the herd. Two hours later the cattle were halted and spruced up cowboys soon headed for relief from the hard, monotonous work and long hours in the saddle.

After exchanging formal greetings and taking the seat offered by the commander of the Army post, Cap put his request. "I'd like to see Jess Sharp, I believe he's serving at this post."

The officer pursed his lips and looked

hard at Cap. "Yes, Sharp's a private here, but as for seeing him that depends on the nature of your business."

Cap hesitated. He put the officer about forty, a regular, stern, brooking no nonsense, but there was a softness about his blue eyes which spoke of a hidden gentleness and Cap judged him to be a fair man whom soldiers respected. Cap knew from his accent that the post commander was from the North and for a moment he wondered if, by giving the true reason for his visit he might gain sympathy from a man whose tanned face was trouble-lined and whose hair was prematurely grey from the horrors of war.

But Cap did not want sympathy, he wanted information. He faced an army man who must have buried all antagonism for the South because now he served on a southern post with Southerners under his command. Cap decided against giving the captain the real purpose of his visit.

"I'm trying to trace two men with

whom Sharp was once friendly," said Cap. The officer's silence signified he expected to hear more. "I had a brother fought with the South; I'm trying to trace him and I believe that Sharp's two acquaintances could help me."

"Seems a reasonable request," the officer approved. "Sharp's in the cells." He saw the surprise on Cap's face. "A case of disobeying an order," he explained. "He'll be tried in four days, but you needn't wait until then. I'll get the sergeant to take you to see him."

"Thanks," replied Cap.

"Sergeant!"

"Sir!" The sergeant entered from the adjoining room.

"Mr Millet would like to see Private Sharp. Escort him to the cell block."

"Yes, sir." The sergeant stood to attention beside the door.

Cap pushed himself from his chair. "Thanks," he said. "I appreciate you letting me speak with Sharp." He held out his hand which the officer took firmly.

"Leave your gun with Private Jenkins in the other office; and any other weapon you may have. Sorry about that, you know how it is when visiting prisoners, can't take any chances."

Cap nodded. It was only what he had expected since receiving the disappointing news that Sharp was in the cells. Revenge on Jess Sharp would have to wait. He'd be easy to trace later even if he was moved from Fort Worth. Cap smiled to himself, little did Sharp know how disobeying an order had prolonged his life. All Cap could do now was to try to get a lead on Walt Mason and Rowdy Martin.

Cap's nerves tightened as they entered the log-built cell-block. In a few moments he would face a man whom he believed raped and murdered his wife. It gripped him with an odd sensation, one he didn't like.

The sergeant passed on the commanding officer's authority for Cap to see Sharp. A few moments' later, Cap watched a man swing from his reclining position to sit on the edge of his bunk in response to the guard's call of, "Sharp, someone to see you!"

There was the age of war in the face of this twenty-four-year-old. He eyed Cap suspiciously from deep-blue eyes, which should have filled with a joy of living in the contentment of a peaceful land but from which youth had been torn by the horrors of a civil war. The sensitivity which had once been the feature of his face was now masked with a hardness which brought belligerence and a contempt of authority.

"Jack Millet." Cap introduced himself, deliberately giving his christian name rather than his more usual nickname which, reflecting his past rank, he figured would bring antagonism and a deliberate blockage to cooperation from Sharp.

"Should I know you?" Sharp's voice was edgy.

"No."

"Well, what you want with me? If it ain't getting me out of this goddamned

Army I don't want to know."

"I'd like your help."

There was mockery in Sharp's harsh laugh. "Help? From me in here?"

"Information. I'm trying to trace Walt Mason and Rowdy Martin. I believe you were with them during the war."

"What you want to know for?" Sharp was suspicious.

"They knew my brother, served with him for a while. I'm trying to trace him, thought they might be able to help."

"Millet." Sharp savoured the name thoughtfully and slowly. "Can't say I ever heard them talk about him."

"Maybe it was before you met them." Cap knew his words were risky. If Sharp had been with Mason and Martin all through the war he would know Cap was lying.

Sharp hesitated then said, "Suppose so. It was towards the end that I palled up with them. Walt and Rowdy were the sensible ones. Got out of the Army as soon as they could; bloody fool me signed on."

"Know where they are?" pressed Cap.

"Rowdy and Walt decided to stick together. Last I heard they were working in Abilene."

Cap could hardly suppress his delight at this news. Things seemed to be working out for him at last. "Thanks," he said. "That's a great help." He turned towards the cell door, and was about to shout for the guard when Sharp stopped him with a question.

"How did you find me?"

"Pete Carter.

"Pete? Couldn't he tell you about Rowdy and Walt?"

"No. He was dead."

Cap's statement startled Sharp. Incredulity crossed his face and his eyes filled with disbelief. "You having me on?"

"No. Bounty hunter brought him into Durango while I was there. Letter from you in his pocket told me you were in Fort Worth."

"Bloody hell, if that ain't my goddamned luck. I was figuring on

Pete busting me out of here and me joining up with him."

Cap ignored Sharp's statement and called for the guard. The guard unlocked the door and, without a backward glance at Sharp, Cap left the cell. He recovered his gun, rode out of the Army post and headed for town.

The civilians had already welcomed the Hash Knife riders eager to find relief from the dry, dusty, all-male trail drive. They were ready to part the cowboy from his money whether he wanted to spend it in the saloon, at the gaming tables or with the calico queens. Spawned on the cotton trade, Fort Worth was not going to be slow to offer its wares to a new source of income, the cowboys trailing longhorns from the south.

After a bath in a tub behind the saloon, Cap decided to have a meal. One of the tables in the cafe was occupied by three Hash Knife riders who acknowledged his nod when he glanced round the room seeking somewhere to sit. He chose an unoccupied table in a corner and ignored the vacant chair beside the Hash Knife men. His action did not go unnoticed and, without thought for a possible explanation, they murmured among themselves about stuck-up Yankees who thought themselves superior because they had won the war.

Cap ordered a steak, medium-rare, and within ten minutes was enjoying its succulent taste along with its accompanying egg and potatoes, a welcome change from Charlie's beans, sourdough and sonofabitch stew. As he ate he relaxed in the knowledge that he had suddenly, after four years, come a long way along his trail of revenge and he knew where he was going.

Lost in his thoughts he was only vaguely aware of the three Hash Knife cowboys leaving. They did not glance in his direction but he gave that no thought. A few moments later a voice disturbed his relaxed mind.

"Mind if I sit here?"

Cap looked up and saw Johnny standing beside the unoccupied chair. He detected a slight edge to the foreman's voice and saw a smouldering annoyance in his eyes. He wondered what irritated Johnny. Maybe he'd lost money at cards or on the dice or maybe some woman hadn't come up to expectations. Whatever — personal problems were no concern of his unless they effected the peace of the drive.

"No. Sit down," replied Cap, leaning back on his chair.

"Thanks." Johnny hung his Stetson on a hook on the wall and dragged the chair from under the table. He ordered his steak medium cooked and Cap asked for apple pie and coffee.

Throughout these few minutes Cap had been studying Johnny and he sensed that whatever had upset Johnny concerned him.

"Something eating you, Johnny?" His eyes met the foreman's firmly as Johnny switched his attention sharply to the trail boss.

"You ignored three Hash Knife cowboys when you came in here." Annoyance flared to the surface.

Cap's eyes widened with surprise. He was stunned by the smallness of the incident which had upset the foreman.

"I nodded to them," replied Cap, his voice cool. "What more do they want? A bloody kiss on the cheek?"

Johnny ignored Cap's attempt at amusement. "There was a vacant seat at their table but you chose to sit here on your own. They sure took it as a slight. I met them just after they left here, it was obvious something was wrong so I got it out of them."

Cap raised his eyes to heaven and sighed with despair. "Holy, bloody Moses what the hell's gotten into your riders. Didn't it occur to those numb-skulls that a man might want to be on his own? Damn it all, Johnny, I'd just come from the fort, from seeing a man whom I believe raped and murdered my wife." Cap's voice was intense, quiet but forceful, ramming home every word, making a piercing impression on Johnny. "And I could do damn all about it, he was in jail, I wanted to be alone to think on what I'd learned from him."

As Cap's words bit into his mind Johnny felt remorse. He cursed himself for being such a fool for not looking further into the incident which had aroused the indignation of his three men. At the same time he realized there was something deeper to what looked trivial on the surface.

"All right, I'm sorry," replied Johnny. "I shouldn't have jumped to conclusions."

"Sure," snapped Cap. "Nor should your three cowpokes. There are two views to everything."

Johnny stiffened. "You're dead right there are." His voice hardened. "You remember that, you didn't just now."

Cap's eyes narrowed. "See here, Johnny . . ."

"No, you see here," cut in Johnny roughly. "I'm foreman of those three boys; you expect me to keep them in hand, well, in return don't you antagonize them."

"Antagonize them? What we got? Babes in arms?" Cap looked disgusted and there was a note of mockery in his tone.

"Hold on. Hear me out." Johnny's voice came sharp, rapier like. "You know we're sitting on a volcano right through this drive, there's black and white, North and South, Yankees and Confederates. That's just asking for one hell of a heap of trouble. It'll take some avoiding before we get to Kansas, but I aim to do my best to keep my boys from stirring it up. I expect you to do the same. Sure, what happened was trivial, well to some eyes but not to others and trivial things can sometimes become big and I figure as trail boss, especially being a Yankee and more so because you brought in a black, you've got to be extra careful not to antagonize." Johnny suddenly stopped then added quietly. "Well there it is. That's sure the longest speech I ever made."

Cap smiled. His eyes softened. The hard steel barrier, which he had put up when he felt his authority was being challenged, came down. "You're sure telling me off, Johnny. No, no, you did perfectly right," he added quickly when he saw Johnny start to defend his action. "I was careless, I let myself get too preoccupied with my thought of revenge. I'll watch it in the future. Can you fix it with your three men?"

"I reckon so. Those three are pretty tolerant. Loyal Hash Knife. They resented you taking the job over me and resented it all the more when they knew you were a Yankee, but they figured, if it was for the good of the Hash Knife, they'd tolerate you. Some of the others — well, that could be a different story."

Cap nodded thoughtfully, then suddenly relaxed and said, "Eat up, Johnny, then join me in a drink. Forget the drive for a couple of hours; it'll keep us fully occupied when we reach the Red River."

"Tricky?" asked Johnny.

"Depends how it's running, but it sure can be one hell of a sonofabitch if it's in that mood."

When trail boss and foreman reached the saloon it was obvious that some of the Hash Knife riders were going to be suffering from bad heads in the morning.

"Will they be fit to ride?" Cap queried.

Johnny grinned. "They'll sit a horse and do a job whatever their state but Charlie's special brew of thick, strong coffee will soon sober them up."

"I guess," laughed Cap, knowing what Charlie's usual coffee was like let alone his special brew.

They spent a pleasant couple of hours, forgetting the hazards of the trail in their beer and cards. When they left the saloon the sky was flamed by the setting sun and the onset of darkness cast gloomy pools of blackness along the alleys off the main street. As they ambled past the end of one of these stretches of blackness, voices laced with threats stopped them.

"Black bastard, you won't go back there in a hurry after we've finished with you." Johnny recognized Clint's voice.

"You don't own that place."

There was no mistaking Josh's voice and in the glance exchanged between Cap and Johnny there was one unspoken word, Trouble.

Johnny would have started forward but Cap placed a restraining hand on his arm.

"We don't, but we figure a white woman's bed is no place for a black."

"Who says I been with a white woman? Who says I ain't been with one of my own kind?"

"'Cos mister, clever, black bastard, there ain't a black woman in the whorehouse — we've been."

"So — ain't it up to her? Who're you to say who she lays for? If she's willing to take my money then all right."

"It ain't all right," Clint's voice was sharp with anger. "No black lays a white woman and gets away with it!"

Clint's words were followed by a dull thud and a gasp of air driven from someone's body.

Cap moved quickly. "Hold it!" His voice rapped out the words harshly, demanding attention.

Clint Forbes and Joe Durham spun round from Josh who was doubled up against the wall holding his stomach and gulping at air.

"Ho, the bloody Yankee's come to help his black brother." Joe's voice was mocking. He had recognized Cap's voice and, unable to distinguish the figure behind him, had concluded it was Wade. "Ain't that dandy, Clint, we've all three. These damned Yankees can pay for killing my brothers."

His hand started to move towards the handle of his Colt protruding from its leather holster, but his fingers never closed on it. They froze when a voice stabbed the darkness from behind Cap.

"Cool it, Joe, or you'll have to take me as well!"

One word thundered into Joe's mind and he sensed Clint stiffen beside him. Johnny!

The Hash Knife foreman was beside Cap as they moved close enough for Joe and Clint to recognize them. Tension flashed as the four men faced each other. Joe and Clint held back by Johnny's presence.

"Bloody hell, man, you know where this nigger's been?" Clint's voice fumed with anger and frustration.

"Sure we heard you," replied Johnny, his tone needle sharp.

"Well then — or do you approve?"

"He's a free man, he goes where he likes," answered Johnny.

"Keep out of this, Johnny," warned Joe testily. "We've got no quarrel with you. Ease off and let us settle this . . ."

"There's nothing to settle, and it does concern me. Anything that might stop us getting the cattle through safely concerns me and it sure looks as if you're trying to spoil our chances."

"But he's been with a white woman," Clint protested.

"So what?" snapped Cap. "If she's willing."

"Doesn't a bloody Yank care about white women?" The taunt came as a half sneer from Joe Durham.

The tension in Cap moved quickly to explosive point. The swiftness of his movement took Joe completely by surprise and he took the full force of Cap's fist in his face. He crashed back against the wall, his whole body jerking with the sudden impact. His knees sagged and his mind blurred until only instinct kept him on his feet. Before anyone could move Cap's Colt was pointing at Joe's stomach.

"More than you know!" The words pierced from a tongue filled with venomous anger.

Johnny was tense, expecting the finger to squeeze the trigger and annihilate Joe who had thrown a taunt not knowing that Cap was eating his heart out because of what had happened to his wife. But the shot never came. Cap kept an ice-cool grip on final feelings which would have pitched him into the role of murderer.

"You've no right to judge me or Josh. He's a man like you, he's biting as much dust as you, he has feelings just like you and if he wants to escape from the hard grind of a trail drive for a short while with a woman then he's just as entitled as you. And you nor anyone else is going to take it out on him if she's been willing; different if she hadn't been. Now git, and be fit to ride in the morning."

The two men hesitated, then, realizing that they could do nothing, made off down the alley to the main street.

Cap watched them then slammed his Colt back into its leather showing his annoyance at crossing paths with two Hash Knife men.

"Thanks, Mister Cap, Mister Johnny."

95

Josh's words were quiet, playing down the situation.

"I reckon you'd better get back to camp," said Cap. "Johnny and I were on our way there; you can ride with us, it might be safer."

# 5

THE sun beat at the Texas earth from a cloudless sky. Realizing that, on a day such as this, the crossing of the Red River would afford some relief to cattle, horses and men, Cap did not hurry the drive but timed it so that the herd would cross about noon, towards the hottest part of the day.

Once he was satisfied with the herd's movement Cap had a few words with Johnny, left him in charge and, taking Clint with him, rode ahead to the river.

"Johnny tells me you're a good swimmer and a fair reader of rivers," said Cap as the two men settled themselves into the ride.

Clint shrugged his shoulders. "If he says so." His tone was unenthusiastic.

"He does, and because I value his

opinion of you I want your help in finding a suitable crossing of the Red River."

"Don't know it," replied Clint. "Never been in these parts before. I hear tell she can be a bastard."

"She can. Let's hope she'll be easy on us."

Clint made no comment and they rode for a considerable distance in silence until Cap broke it with a question. "Why do you hate blacks?"

Clint turned his head sharply and met Cap's questioning eyes with a smouldering look which intensified with feeling as he met question with question. "Why are you a nigger lover?"

"I ain't a nigger lover!" rapped Cap testily. Clint saw a momentary flash of anger in Cap's eyes but then it was gone, brought sharply under control by a man determined not to be provoked. "They're men the same as you and me. I respect them because they are, I respect their feelings but that don't mean I'm a nigger lover. That implies I prefer their company to that of whites and that ain't so. I judge by what I see in both cases."

"Respect their feelings!" There was contempt in Clint's voice. "You wouldn't say that if your sister had been raped by two bloody niggers!"

Cap was startled by this revelation. Clint and he had something in common. He could go some way to understanding how Clint felt.

"I'm sorry," he said quietly.

"There's no need to offer your sympathy to me. Be sorry for yourself treating those black bastards as equals."

"You can't condemn a whole race for the actions of two."

"They're all the same."

"White men have raped. Do you hate all whites? If white men had raped your sister would you condemn all whites?"

"Blacks are different. They should never have had their freedom. You Yankees will have a lot to answer for when the blacks get drunk with the idea that they are as good as us."

99

"Aren't they? All men are equal."

"Like hell they are."

Cap knew he would get nowhere arguing with Clint. The hatred was too ingrained, just as his hatred of four white men was engraved on his heart but he didn't condemn outright everyone else of the same colour.

The first sound of running water reached them and put an end to the subject. The river! As one they stabbed their horses forward and put them into a gallop. A few minutes later with the roar of fast flowing water in their ears, they surveyed the prospects from the top of a forty-foot bluff above the Red River.

"No good along this section. Down-stream?"

Clint nodded. "We'll try that way first. If the river widens it will shallow and slow, maybe enough to give us a crossing." The two men turned their horses along the top of the reddish bluffs. "Glad we ain't got her in that mood," added Clint, indicating tree timber and drift wood left at precarious angles on ledges some five feet above the present waterline.

Half a mile further on the banks of the river closed sending the water roaring and boiling for a quarter of a mile through a narrow gap.

"That'll be one hell of a place when the river's running high," commented Clint.

Cap nodded. His face showed concern. He hoped he wasn't going to have to divert the herd too far off its present heading, detours consumed precious time.

Beyond the gap the river widened but it took another three miles before it showed any real move in their favour. Sensing they were nearing what they sought the two men moved their mounts faster.

The bluffs began to lower and move back from the river allowing it to widen until, although it still ran swiftly, its venom and turbulance were gone.

Clint eyed the river critically until

he reached a position where the ground dropped only five feet some forty yards back from the river, leaving a gentler slope to the water.

"Reckon we might try here," said Clint stopping his horse close to the water's edge.

Cap reined in beside Clint. He turned in his saddle and surveyed the ground over which the cattle would approach the river. "Looks like a good entrance," he commented. "Right, let's try it." He settled himself in the saddle again and put his horse into the water with Clint alongside him.

Urging the animals gently forward the two men moved further and further into the water. About twenty yards out they felt their horses' hooves leave the bottom and the motion of swimming quiver through the muscular bodies. With necks stretched forward and nostrils strained above the water, the animals made steady progress.

The faster flowing water towards midstream began to make itself felt and strengthened in its attempt to sweep them downstream. The horses strained against it, fighting to keep moving towards the safety of the opposite bank. Clint slipped from the saddle, relieving the horse of his weight. His hand closed round the saddle-horn while his free hand helped to fight the tugging river. Cap copied Clint's action and the two horses, feeling some of their burden ease and sensing their riders' desire to help, summoned extra power to contest the water which sought to destroy them.

For what seemed an eternity they appeared to make no progress against the clutching, tugging river which threatened to tumble them downstream to their deaths. Water swirled around them, buffeting and sweeping with a strength filled with a determination not to be denied. Men and animals fought, matching strength with power. Slowly the bank came nearer. The river fought harder then suddenly seemed to give up and men and animals found themselves in shallow water where the pull was less noticeable. They felt their mastery over the river which had threatened to sweep them to oblivion. When their horses' hooves gripped the bed of the shallowing river both men left go of the saddles and swam the rest of the way, while the horses, freed from the menacing water, scrambled up the bankside snorting and shaking themselves.

Cap and Clint, with water streaming from their saturated clothes, stumbled from the river and scrambled up to the dryness of the soft ground beyond the water's edge. They flopped down, sprawling on their backs, drawing great gulps of air into their aching lungs.

"It'll be tough." Cap's words came in short staccatto gasps.

"Sure will," replied Clint.

They lay in silence while the heaving of their chests subsided and the sun drew the wetness from their clothes.

Cap sat up and looked at the river. "You bastard," he muttered at the swirling waters which seemed to throw out a mocking challenge. "But we'll beat you." He turned to Clint as the cowboy sat up. "Figure we can do it?"

Clint hesitated, weighing his judgement carefully as his critical eyes examined every facet of the barrier which if it had its way would prevent the Hash Knife herd from progressing north.

"Sure," replied Clint, his judgement made. "It'll be damned tricky but if everyone keeps their head there's no reason why we can't get the complete herd across safely."

Cap nodded. "Good. I'd rather cross here if we can otherwise I figure we'll have a long detour."

"Guess so," agreed Clint.

"Right, let's tackle the Red again," said Cap, scrambling to his feet.

The two men hurried to their horses which were nuzzling the ground a short distance away. Once in the saddle the riders put their mounts at the water. Knowing the strengths and weaknesses of the river they reached the south bank of the Red River without undue anxiety.

From a rise to the east of the herd, Cap viewed it critically. Satisfied with what he saw and knowing there was no danger, he pulled the men in for instructions about the crossing which faced them.

"It's going to be tricky but it can be done," he told them. "There's a deal of swimming so get your best horses. The steers will have to be held in check especially when they smell that water. If they hit that river hard it could be fatal. Charlie, I want the chuck-wagon over first and positioned about half a mile from the river. It'll have to be floated over so Clint, you take two men and fix that, then hold on to help Josh over with the remuda. Josh, you hold it in readiness on the other side in case any more horses are wanted. The rest of us will just ease the herd along. We should be able to make the crossing just after noon." He looked round his men. "Any questions?" There were none, and with Cap's "get to it," the men broke up to their various jobs.

Clint took Joe Durham and Fox Honeyman, and Johnny quickly made the necessary adjustments to the men riding with the herd.

As Clint, Joe and Fox rode off with Charlie, Johnny questioned Cap's decision. "Do you think it wise to leave those three to help Josh?"

"I've seen the Red; they'll be too occupied to think of other things, and working close with Josh might just help to ease the animosity. Besides you said Clint's the best swimmer and knows rivers so he's got to be there."

Johnny made no comment.

Once at the river Charlie unhitched his mules and took them across using Joe's horse, while the three cowboys quickly utilised available timber and made a raft for the chuck wagon. Rough and crude though it was it served its purpose and, once they had manhandled the wagon on to the raft, they poled it across the river, allowing the current to swing them downstream. On reaching the north bank, after only one anxious moment in midstream, when the river threatened to take over, they soon had the wagon ashore.

When the mules were hitched to the wagon the three cowboys left Charlie to find his own camp site while they carried the raft to a suitable launching point upstream. Clint judged the position well and, as they poled themselves across, the river carried them downstream to a place close to where they had left their horses. The raft was turned loose to be whirled away by the river, and the men climbed into the saddles and rode to the top of the bank.

Clint reined his horse and narrowed his eyes to the distant dust-cloud which signified the position of the remuda. "Let the black bastard bring them in himself," he commented and swung from the saddle.

Joe and Fox followed suit and the three men relaxed on the ground awaiting Josh's arrival.

"You still figuring on fixing the

black?" asked Joe.

"Sure."

"Well, three of us can do for him. You ain't inclined towards blacks are you, Fox?"

"Sure ain't, but I'm not so sure about killing . . . "

"It'll be an accident, Fox, an accident," broke in Clint.

"So long as it doesn't spoil the chances of the herd getting through," replied Fox with some doubt. "I don't think . . . "

"How the hell can the death of one no-good black jeopardise the safety of the herd. I'll fix him; you just keep your mouth shut."

Clint kept his attention on the approach of the remuda and moved only when he judged it was time they intervened in its progress to the river.

Josh was weaving his way back and forth across the front of the lead horses, trying desperately to hold them from breaking into a run for the water. Clint smiled to himself when he saw the worried concern of a man who knew that at any moment the situation might get out of hand. He knew Josh had sweated on the possibility of losing some of the remuda.

"Where you bastards been?" yelled Josh angrily as he wheeled his horse.

"Mind your tongue, nigger-boy," shouted Clint with a grin which was not friendly. "Getting scared of them horses?"

"If they run for the river we'll lose some and that ain't going to be to Mister Cap's liking." Josh checked a horse which was showing some determination to break away and pulled his own mount round to glare angrily at Clint, almost daring him not to help.

Clint met the look and nearly took up the challenge. Then he eased the tension.

"Ease up, nigger-boy. We'll see these horses safely over not for your Mister Cap but for the Hash Knife." He turned to Joe and Fox. "Keep them in check.

Nigger-boy and I will ease them into the river."

Joe and Fox moved to their positions, one on either side of the remuda, from where they could bring pressure to bear on the animals and give them little room to move except straight ahead where they were held to a pace dictated by Clint and Josh.

"See, nigger-boy, it's easy," grinned Clint, once the horses had settled down. He put a tone of superiority into his voice knowing it would not be lost on Josh who was seething under the taunt of nigger every time Clint threw it. Clint sensed Josh straining to hold back his temper. He wished he would let it erupt, maybe he'd get a chance to kill in self-defence.

But the chance never came for suddenly they were at the edge of the bank with the slope stretching before them.

"Take 'em straight in!" yelled Clint. He had led the remuda to a point from which he estimated that they would be swung by the current to a convenient exit on the opposite bank. He quickened the pace to satisfy the restive horses while still holding them in check as they neared the water. "This side, with me, nigger," he called, drawing Josh across so that they were both downstream of the lead horses and ready to prevent them moving too far under the force of the current.

Exerting pressure on the lead horses as they entered the water they kept them moving in the desired direction. Joe and Fox remained on the edge of the river funnelling the horses into the water and preventing them from spreading out along the river bank. Once he was satisfied that the situation was in hand, Clint signalled to Joe and Fox to start crossing for he knew he would need their help alongside the remuda once the lead horses hit swimming water.

The river swirled around them creeping higher and higher with every step. Clint and Josh shouted and cajoled, keeping the leaders moving. The moment two of them showed signs of panic Clint was at them forcing them on until suddenly they found themselves swimming and they settled down to battle the fast flowing current.

Clint glanced back and saw Josh slip from the saddle to ease the burden for his horse. He hesitated a moment before doing the same and that moment brought him close to Josh as he slid into the water.

The horses were swimming strongly but the force of the current was sweeping them downstream and the whole remuda was swung out across the river in a big arc. The four men kept their horses close alongside the remuda forcing it to greater exertions against the current. Clint momentarily checked his horse. It was an almost imperceptible movement, one which only someone watching closely would have seen and the other three men were too preoccupied to be doing that.

Clint's and Josh's horses crashed against each other. In the moment of fright Clint left go of the saddle-horn and let the water swirl at him appearing to drag him away. He grabbed Josh as if to save himself. The negro felt the grasp, felt the tug. He tried desperately to hold on to his saddle-horn but the pull was too great and he was forced to release his grip.

Both men went underwater and Josh felt himself pulled down as Clint fought against him to regain the surface. Josh tried to release Clint's grip. His lungs felt as if they would burst as he tried to hold on to the small amount of air he had when he went under. Clint broke the surface and in a quick glance saw the remuda was still moving well about ten yards away. He increased his pressure on Josh, determined to hold him under. In that moment Josh realized he was fighting for his life, this was no accident otherwise he would have been alongside Clint gulping air into his lungs. Water stung at his eyes and his ears and his mind pounded as if to burst. He got a grip on the hand pressing on his right shoulder and in that small triumph found an extra power to his efforts to free himself. His broad fingers tightened to the point of pain. As angry hurt stabbed along Clint's arm he felt a jerk and found he no longer had pressure on Josh's shoulder. Free from being thrust down in the water Josh kicked sharply for the surface. At the same time he used his grip on Clint's arm to add momentum to his upward surge.

Turbulent waters scattered as Josh's head burst to the surface and Clint went under. Josh gasped hard, drawing air deep into his straining lungs. He shook water from his eyes and face and through the blurring, swirl of water he saw Clint resurface.

Josh, fiercely determined to survive, seized his chance and struck hard at Clint before the white man could regain his balance and allow the demonical urge to destroy black to take the upper hand again. But even as Josh lashed out, the river buffeted Clint, knocking him off balance, and the blow merely caught his shoulder. Clint grabbed Josh's arm and the two men grappled amid the turbulence of the heaving water. The swirling river gripped them with clinging fingers and tossed them closer to the bank. As they tumbled over, still locked in each other's grip, their feet dragged at the riverbed and each of them struggled to get a firm stance.

Clint found himself upright, still holding Josh's shirt in his left hand, as the negro staggered on the roughness beneath his feet. Clint's clenched right fist drove hard into Josh's face with a force which jerked him free of Clint's grip. He staggered backwards and crashed heavily in the shallower water. Clint's grin of triumph came as, with chest heaving, he pushed himself against the water to get at Josh again.

With his head pounding from the blow, Josh struggled to keep his mind sharp and his senses alert knowing that to succumb would mean the end. He forced himself to his feet and, with water swirling round his thighs, his arms hanging slackly by his sides, he half crouched, gulping at the air and waiting for Clint's next attack.

Their eyes locked on each other and hatred of each other's colour stabbed between them through the water which streamed down their sodden faces from their sodden hair. That hatred was suddenly pierced by a scream of terror ripping across the river. Clint stopped and turned.

He stared in shocked bewilderment at the maelstrom of horses and man being swallowed by the river. He could only guess that one of the remuda had lost its footing and crashed against Fox Honeyman's mount, unseating the rider and tossing him to the river which cut short his frightening cry.

With Clint's back to him Josh saw his chance. His concentration on Clint had been so intense that he was only vaguely aware of what had happened to Fox but suddenly, when Fox appeared on the surface it bit deep.

Fox's arms flayed but had no effect against the buffeting. He was being swept away at the mercy of the river.

As Clint started to turn back to face the negro, Josh flung himself forward, knocked Clint out of the way and launched himself into deeper water. He started to swim strongly, hoping to cut off the helpless man before he was swept passed him. The gap between them narrowed but Josh realized he would not make it. He turned with the current while maintaining his swim. His power, coupled with that of the river, took him well ahead of Fox. Josh turned and battled against the rush of water as he quickly sized up his position.

Fox was coming at him fast. Then suddenly he was upon Josh. The negro grabbed. He felt his arm lock with Fox's as he tumbled over the impact. For a few moments the river took command, sweeping them downstream. Then both men fought against it with their free arm to bring some sort of stability to their movement through the wild waters.

The current swung towards the bank carrying the two men with it.

"Grab!" shouted Josh as they were swept towards some overhanging branches.

Both men grasped at the branches and halted their progress with a suddeness which seemed to tear their arms from their sockets. They hung on, each supporting the other, while they drank air into their river-beaten bodies.

"Thanks," gasped Fox. He wanted to say more but found the effort too much.

Josh nodded. He weighed up their situation. "We can work our way to the bank."

He began to inch his way along the branch keeping his pace to that manageable by Fox. Muscles and arms ached with the pull of their bodies but gradually they moved nearer the bank leaving the river to rush on its torment at losing two victims. Once above the bank beyond the water, Josh dropped to the ground. As he straightened to help Fox he noticed the cowboy's leg was badly crushed into a blood oozing mess. He took Fox's weight and lowered him gently to the ground.

"Lay still, we'll get you to Charlie as soon as possible."

Fox nodded. "And thanks again for saving my life."

Josh said nothing but turned his attention to the river. The remuda was still strung out in a great arc but the lead horses were already coming out on to the bank about two hundred yards upstream. Joe Durham was setting his horse along the bank in his direction. Josh looked across the turbulant Red River. Clint was still standing in the same place in the water near the opposite bank, as if he had been transfixed by the near-tragedy.

Loathing and contempt seethed in Josh for the man who was prepared to let one of his own kind be swept to his death while he sought revenge to satisfy his hatred for the blacks.

Josh sighed and turned to face the approaching Joe Durham. "Why the hell did I bother?" Josh muttered to himself between tight lips. "There could have been two bloody whites less."

"You all right?" As he pulled his horse to a churning stop in the soft ground, Joe Durham's concern was directed more at Fox than at Josh, a fact not lost on the negro. A black's life was cheap; it was expendable. Josh was not surprised at Joe's attitude, even though his hatred was directed more at Yankees for in pursuing the blame for his brother's death to the ultimate he condemned the negroes for being the cause of the war.

"His leg's badly smashed, he needs attention from Charlie," said Josh.

Joe, seeming to ignore Josh's words, looked directly at Fox. Fox met his gaze and flashed back a look of annoyance. Angry words came to his lips in defence of the man who had saved his life but he curbed them knowing they could cause further disruption whereas the situation needed taking in hand.

"Get Josh's horse, I see it and Clint's have come ashore. He can take me to Charlie. You can take Clint's horse back across the Red."

Joe pulled his horse round and in a few moments was gathering up the reins of Josh's horse. He lead it back and threw the reins to Josh but directed his question to Fox.

"Will you be all right?"

"Sure," replied Fox.

Joe rode off without a word.

Josh helped Fox into the saddle and swung up behind him. They were not long in finding Charlie who showed his concern at seeing two men, one with a badly smashed leg, both wet through and both riding one horse.

"Leg crushed between two horses," explained Josh as he dropped to the ground.

"And you ain't been cuddling a gal to get a face like that," observed Charlie as he reached to help Fox.

"Forget that, Charlie. I'm all right," replied Josh.

They lowered Fox gently to the ground. "He ain't telling you he saved my life," he told Charlie.

Charlie shot a questioning glance at Josh who ignored Fox's remark. "Guess I'll be getting back to the remuda." He grabbed the horse's reins and swung up into the saddle, sending the horse away before Charlie could ask any more questions.

When Josh approached the river he saw that the horses were still following the leaders out of the water and away from the river bank. He saw no sign of Joe or Clint, and set about moving the remuda a suitable distance so that the herd would not be impeded when it made the crossing.

Anticipating the return of the men from the river Cap rode in advance of the slow moving herd above which dust hung heavily, untouched by any movement of air, held still by the oppressive heat. He knew men, horses and steers would welcome the water but he did not want to hurry them until he knew that the remuda was safely across.

He sighted two riders approaching at a brisk pace. Cap's lips tightened. Why only two? He needed every man to get the herd across safely. Cap spurred his horse to meet them.

The three men stopped on meeting. Clint needed no voiced questions they were there in Cap's grey eyes. He answered them. "Remuda's over safely, only a little trouble when one horse lost its footing just before hitting deep water. Fell against Fox who was swept away. Josh saved him but Fox has a damaged leg. Josh took him to Charlie. Should have no difficulty with the herd."

Cap nodded. He was in possession of the facts, they needed no comment. He turned his horse and as the three riders headed for the herd he said, "Take over at point and send Wade and Rod back to flank. We'll push 'em a bit harder."

They put their horses into a gallop to their respective positions, with Cap passing the order to hurry the steers and informing Johnny of Clint's report.

Although the pace quickened, the trail riders had no difficulty in keeping the steers under control but it needed all their skill to prevent a stampede once the smell of water reached the herd.

Cap and Johnny joined the point riders and closed in on the lead steers, keeping them tight and compact so that they could take to the water on a narrow front. The steers revelled in the cool wetness after the dry heat as the cowboys urged them deeper and deeper into the water. Dust swirled high released into upward flight by the hooves tearing at the approach to the Red River. Hash Knife riders choked on the dust and sweated under the pounding of the high sun while they wheeled and turned their mounts keeping the cattle moving and holding the herd from spreading out.

Cap was everywhere, in the river and out, supervising, encouraging and criticising, keeping the men to the task as he wanted it carrying out. He felt some relief when he saw the lead steers take to the bank and emerge from the turbulance and strength of the Red River safely. Cattle were strung out across the river and cowboys had their work cut out holding them to the course which would take them to safety. Occasionally a piercing cry rent the air above the sound of the bellowing cattle still on the bank as some steer was overpowered by the river and dragged away to its death. Cap was concerned for each one but there was little anyone could do once an animal was in the grip of the river. He counted himself lucky that only five steers were lost in this way. The last steer found its footing and thrust against the flowing water to scramble its spraying way on to the dry bank. It paused, shook itself free of some of the wetness and moved off to graze lazily with the rest of the herd which had been allowed to spread out as it willed under the watchful eyes of the riders. Relieved of the drive and the crossing of the Red River the animals would not stray far.

Cap relaxed in the saddle satisfied at a hard job well done. A physical and psychological barrier had been crossed. He had sensed the nervousness of the Hash Knife cowboys when they approached the river but they had worked hard, become absorbed in the job and lost the tension. It showed in their relaxed postures, the smiles on their faces and in the chaffing banter which passed between them as they headed for the chuck wagon and Charlie's food.

Cap sent his horse into a steady walking pace towards the remuda grazing peacefully ahead. He saw Josh saddling a horse and turning his mount towards him stabbed it into a trot.

"Hi, Josh, hear you did a mighty brave thing," Cap called as he pulled his horse to a halt behind the black man.

Josh turned from tightening the cinch. He grinned but saw it was not returned. Instead a surprised look of disbelief stared down at him from the man in the saddle.

"What the hell happened to you?" Cap's voice was a mixture of surprise and demand.

"Nothing, boss. It was an accident."

"Accident be damned," returned Cap sharply. He'd seen enough fist marks on a mans face to recognize them now.

"Forget it, Mister Cap."

"Why should I?" Cap had already guessed that the trouble could have happened only when the remuda was crossing the river. He'd been a fool to entrust the job of helping Josh to Clint.

"The herd's the important thing," replied Josh. He turned back to complete the saddling, wanting to put an end to the questioning.

Cap knew he would get no more out of the negro. With his lips set in a grim line, he pulled his horse round and sent it quickly away in the direction of the chuck wagon.

Cowboys were lining up for their stew when Cap reached the camp site. When he swung from the saddle he made straight for Fox who was lying in the shade of the chuck wagon.

"How's the leg, Fox?" asked Cap as he dropped on one knee beside the crippled man.

"Not as bad as it looked," replied Fox. "Charlie did a good job of cleaning it up. He figures there's only one break."

Cap lifted the blanket laid loosely over Fox's leg and approved of the way Charlie had set it.

"Take care, Fox, and you should come to no harm. You'll have to ride in the wagon." He rearranged the blanket carefully then looked hard at Fox.

"What happened at the crossing?" he asked.

"Horse lost its footing and . . . "

"I don't mean the accident," cut in

Cap. "Josh has fist marks on his face. He won't talk so I'm asking you."

"I don't know," replied Fox. "I was too busy before the accident to notice."

"Or too loyal to Hash Knife riders to say." Irritated, Cap pushed himself to his feet. He was determined to get to the bottom of the trouble. He glanced round the Hash Knife cowboys and saw Clint Forbes and Joe Durham eating their meal with Johnny. He crossed quickly to them. "You seen Josh?" He directed his question at Johnny.

"No."

"Then you ain't seen the fist marks on his face," rapped Cap. "Put there by these two no doubt."

He glared angrily at Clint and Joe.

Clint stopped eating and looked up slowly at Cap. "You accusing?" he asked.

"No, I'm saying," replied Cap testily. "That bloody nigger came bleating to you."

"No. But the evidence is on his face and he couldn't have got it any other time but when you were there with the remuda. You were right, Johnny, it was a mistake to send Clint to help Josh over the Red." His voice was rising with his anger. "He's no good to this drive." He glared at Clint. "You can head back to the Hash Knife. I'm not having the safety of the herd threatened by you."

"Or is it Josh you're thinking of?" Joe Durham was on his feet, his words lashing at Cap with the hatred pouring from his eyes.

"You're no better than Clint, so you can ride with him."

The tension was heightening to explosive point. Joe Durham was just hitching to gun down a Yankee and Clint was ready to back him.

"Hold it!" Johnny cut in to take a hold on the situation. He guessed that Clint had gone for Josh, and Clint hadn't denied it but there was something far more important to Johnny. "We can't afford to weaken our drive by losing two drivers."

"We'll manage," replied Cap testily.

"Everyone will have to put in more effort."

The tension in the small group had spread itself to the whole camp. Cowboys had stopped eating, put down their plates, scrambled to their feet and directed their attention to the trouble which was quickly involving them all.

"Can't be done." Johnny's words came firm and in their precise quietness there was every indication that Johnny was not going to be moved from his opinion. "You're forgetting Fox, we're three riders short and you can't take the herd on that short."

"We can." Cap stared coldly at Johnny.

"You'll be jeopardising the herd far more if you try it than if you keep Clint and Josh with us," rapped Johnny.

Cap ignored Johnny's observation and turned to Clint and Joe. "I'm running this drive. Now git!"

Joe Durham's hand moved nearer the butt of his gun. Clint's eyes went cold. Cap Millet was bucking their foreman.

132

He glanced at Johnny. They could take this no good Yankee here and now. Johnny read the signs.

"Back off, Joe. You too, Clint." Johnny's order lashed at the two men and they realized that Johnny would draw against them if they attempted to settle the matter with guns. "I don't give a damn about your stupid prejudices but I won't have them threatening the safety of this herd." He turned to Cap. "Nor will I have a crazy dismissal of two men at this stage of the drive. It's bad enough losing Fox but two more just as we're facing Indian territory is asking for trouble. If they go the rest of the Hash Knife goes too!"

Johnny's announcement stunned Cap. He had not expected the Hash Knife foreman to take this sort of stand.

"What will Frank say when he knows you deserted the herd?"

"What will he say when he knows you put the herd in danger, that you created the situation?" countered Johnny.

133

"Clint created this situation not me," replied Cap.

"Frank didn't want you to bring Josh along, but you insisted."

"You know the reason."

"That could have waited until the herd was safely delivered. We're getting nowhere fast. Three of you can't take the herd through so you'd better take another think." Johnny wanted to get the matter settled.

Cap eyed him coldly. "You bastard," he muttered. "You've got me. I reckon you would do just as you say so I'd better reinstate these two coyotes." His eyes narrowed as he looked at Clint and Joe who had relaxed and were grinning at their triumph. "If you two step out of line Johnny will be in trouble 'cos of now I'm making him responsible for you and what you do." He turned and strode to his horse, swung into the saddle and rode to the remuda where Josh had been joined by Wade unaware of the trouble in the camp.

The silence in the camp as Cap rode

away was broken a few moments later by a raucous laugh and "That's put bloody Mister Cap in his place."

Cowboys smiled and in the relaxation turned to Johnny. "Nice work, Johnny." "That's showing him, boss." But the foreman was unsmiling.

"He's put you in your place." Johnny's anger was directed at Clint and Joe. "You walk straight from now on or you'll have me to answer to. This herd is going through and anybody that messes up its chances will have Johnny Hines to face. Losing these steers will ruin the Hash Knife and you'll all be out of a job. Can't you get that into your thick skulls. Sit on your personal feelings until the end of the drive."

The Hash Knife riders winced under Johnny's scathing tongue. They knew that he was not a man to tangle with and that from now on everyone's actions would be scrutinised thoroughly.

"And what happens at the end of the drive?" asked Clint.

"I couldn't care less. Once I have

the money for Frank then I head for Texas. I hope you'll all head back for your jobs; I'd like to keep you as a crew."

"What happens to the nigger and the two nigger-loving Yankees?" asked Clint.

"They were hired for the drive only. Their jobs end then."

"And maybe something else," grinned Clint. "With me, Joe?"

"Sure," grinned Joe. "We can wait."

"That'll be your affair," replied Johnny when he saw their looks question where he stood. "If you want to tangle with those three after the drive that's your lookout, but my word to you is don't underestimate Cap Millet."

"We can handle him," grinned Clint, "and his side-kicks." He glanced round the cowboys. "Don't anyone get the idea of tipping him off." His eyes settled on Johnny. "And that goes for you too."

# 6

"WE'LL be lucky if we cut through Indian territory without any trouble," Cap warned the men before they set the cattle in motion away from the Red River. "Keep extra vigilance, especially at night. If the Indians don't get right down hostile they'll try to stampede the cattle in the dark and pick up the strays."

"Heard tell the Army were policing the territory," Charlie put in.

"Sure, supposed to be. Ain't properly organized yet," replied Cap. "I figure you all think like me, you'd rather rely on your own weapons and initiative than sit around hoping the Army'll show up."

There was a murmur of agreement from the Hash Knife cowboys and with that approval Cap got the drive under way.

137

As the cattle streamed into a long, snaking line, three steers who had established their dominance early in the drive moved into the lead. The cowboys allowed them to dictate the pace for they had already realized that the rest of the herd followed and paced themselves to these three. They needed little cajoling to keep moving and Cap, though he would have liked to cross the next three hundred miles as quickly as possible respected the pace for it meant that the cattle would not run weight off, an important consideration when it came to selling at the end of the drive.

For four days the cattle trailed through mile upon mile of seared brown grass which stretched its undulation far to the horizon without a sign of an Indian. Dust rose high and Cap knew it would not have gone unseen. He constantly urged the men to keep vigilant for they tended to drift into a relaxing complacancy as each succeeding day remain trouble-free.

The thrum of hooves made Cap look up from his plate during the fifth noonday stop since crossing the Red River. He narrowed his eyes against the glare of the sun and saw Jim Lovell who had been riding loose herd with Red Fletcher heading for the camp at a brisk pace.

"Indians!" he called as he brought his mount to a dust stirring halt.

Tension immediately gripped the camp. All eyes turned on Cap.

"How many?" he asked sharply.

"Three, old man and two young bucks."

Cap handed his plate to Charlie. "Come on, Johnny," he called. "Rest of you finish your grub, this ain't a raid."

Cap followed by the foreman ran to his horse and in a few moments they were riding with Jim in the direction of the herd.

They joined Red who had moved to a position between the herd and the Indians still a quarter of a mile away.

Cap watched them approaching. He saw an old man, a blanket around his hunched shoulders in spite of the heat, giving the picture of weariness. The two young men riding one on either side of him, looked dejected and sapped of all strength, but Cap's feeling of mistrust, which was turning to sympathy, was heightened when they were near enough for him to see their eyes. They were bright, sharp and alert.

The Indians stopped their ponies five yards from the white men.

"Beef?" the old Indian begged. He indicated his stomach. "Hung . . . ry." He indicated the two young men. "Sons hung . . . ry." Still pointing to his two companions he went on, "Squaws hung . . . ry, papoose hung . . . ry."

Cap nodded, keeping his eyes fixed firmly on the Indians. He indicated that he would give them one steer and said to Red "Cut one out for them."

Red wheeled his horse and a few moments later drove a young steer to the Indians. Smiles cut across their faces and the old made a sign of his thanks. One of the young Indians drew a knife but the old man stopped him and nodded in the direction from which they had come as he spoke a few sharp words.

The Indians turned their horses and made off, driving the steer before them.

"Poor sods," muttered Jim.

"Don't sympathize with those three," said Cap. "They were no more hungry than I am. They were looking us over."

"You figure there'll be big trouble?" asked Johnny.

"Well, last year's drive got through by giving a beef each day to the Indians but I don't figure on doing that so we'll have to see what happens. Keep the men alert, Johnny."

The drive got under way again and when the herd was bedded down for the night Cap put on extra men to ride night herd but all was quiet. The next day the same three Indians appeared once again pleading hunger and asking for another steer. Cap would not give way and made every sign to show that he had already given them one and that should last the family a few days.

Before turning in for the night Cap ordered every man to leave a horse saddled and be ready to ride in an instant. He slept uneasily and was awake an hour before dawn when he heard a movement amongst the cattle.

He was on his feet quickly and moved swiftly round the sleeping men waking them. Leaving one man with Charlie, Cap led the rest to the herd. The cattle quickly settled down again but although he saw no Indians Cap felt certain that they were about and that he had averted a stampede by this show of alertness and strength.

The herd maintained its progress throughout the next week without another visit from the Indians but Cap was not to be lulled into a false sense of security. He continually urged the Hash Knife men to keep alert but the continuing monotony of the drive under the hot sun sapped their strength of concentration.

Sleep became overpowering and the watchful, patient Indians timed their attack to perfection. They were among the cattle before the night riders realized it. The surprise was complete and the Indians, frightening the steers, sent them into a stampeding run.

The bellowing and the pound of hooves brought Cap springing from his blankets. He cursed to himself as he grasped the situations and knew the Indians had outwitted them. His loud yells brought cowboys from their sleep and sent them racing for their horses. They were into the saddles and racing after the cattle almost before they realized what was happening. Then they were alert, keyed up to the finest point in their attempt to stop the stampede and save the herd.

Six Indians who had succeeded in moving into the herd without being detected and had sent the steers into their wild run, raced across the prairie to their companion who held their ponies in readiness. But there was no need for immediate escape, the cowboys were too occupied trying to control the herd for them to bother about Indians. Laughing and congratulating themselves, they sprang on to their ponies and watched the pandemonium for a few minutes before setting their mounts into a steady movement following the stampeding herd. The cowboys would save the majority of the steers but they would be satisfied to pick up the strays.

The riders, following Cap's orders, ranged themselves along the right side of the herd. The ground pounded with the beat of earth-tearing hooves as they attempted to outride the stampeding steers.

The horses responded to the urging of voice and muscle and steadily overtook the lead animals. Cap was out in front with Joe Durham close to him. Ten yards behind them Wade Lawson just held the lead on Johnny with the rest of the outfit bunched not far behind.

Clouds scudded from the moon leaving the sky clear and the prairie bathed in brilliant moonlight. A quick, backward glance showed Cap that the riders were well placed and barring mishaps they should be able to get at grips with the stampede without too much trouble.

Five minutes more of hard riding brought Cap and Joe alongside the lead steers ready to put pressure on them. Flaying hooves closed as Cap edged nearer the heaving cattle. Joe eyed Cap's move and sent his horse closer to the herd. The nearest lead steers, startled by the yelling intrusion of the two riders, tried to turn away. Horn crashed against horn as steer bumped steer bringing pressure to bear on the rest of the leaders. Sensing that they had started a move which would turn the herd, Cap and Joe moved closer to the stampeding hooves whiles the rest of the outfit urged the herd to follow the arcing run of the leaders.

The run curved more. If only they

could keep this up Cap knew they had won, the herd would turn in on itself and circle until it had run itself out. He kept up the pressure on the leaders knowing the whole outfit was playing its part behind him. Joe eyed Cap and moved closer, his attention diverted from the onrush of the steers to the galloping mount of his trail boss.

A cool calculating calmness steeled inside him in spite of his mind pounding along with the drumming of the hooves. What better chance to get even with the damned Yankees who had taken his brother's life? An accident could happen easily and with everyone's attention directed to stopping the herd who would be able to say what had happened?

He edged nearer Cap. The pressure they were exerting was having its effect. The leaders were turning. Joe's nerves tensed. It was now or never.

There was a sudden clash of horseflesh. The two animals whinneyed with fright. Joe's horse sheered away as Cap's was driven hard against the nearest steer. Taken completely unawares, Cap lost control. His horse jerked to find its own safety as its hooves momentarily lost their grip. Once they bit the earth again the animal leaped forward almost unseating its rider. Feeling himself going Cap strained against the pull, regained his balance and went with the horse as it tore away from the death flaying hooves of the steers. Cap let it run for a few moments then took it under control, gently soothing away its fears. It was all over in a matter of minutes but in that time some of the steers, feeling the pressure ease, broke back into their straight run away from the turning leaders.

Joe's horse had carried him some distance ahead and, as he turned it sharply, it lost its footing and crashed to the ground pitching its rider heavily from the saddle. Partially dazed, Joe pushed himself to his feet. He staggered, turned for his horse only to see the frightened animal already up again galloping away from the breakaway steers. Joe froze. He was right in their path. Death pounded towards him in the shape of mutilating hooves. Terror gripped the cowboy.

Suddenly he was galvanized into action as the instinct for preservation took over. He raced to get out of the way of frightening wall of steers thundering towards him. He knew it was a forlorn chance but he had to try.

Awareness of a horse and rider in full gallop, ahead of the steers, coming towards him came hazily and then the possibilities of rescue hit Joe with an impact which brought alertness to a new situation. He eyed the rider's approach, turned the same way and slowed as he looked back over his shoulder. The horse was close; the rider checked its run; he leaned from the saddle and Joe grasped at the outstretched hand. The man gripped him under the armpit and as he straightened and heaved upwards Joe helped the momentum by pushing hard on the ground.

Even as Joe swung up behind him and grappled to gain his balance, the rider was urging his horse back into full gallop to carry them away from the death flaying hooves. And Joe was aware that his rescuer was Cap.

Cautious not to make his turn too violent Cap eased his horse from the path of the breakaway steers. Once clear he eased his mount to a stop. Joe shivered as the pounding hooves passed close by, drumming the nearness of death into his mind. But for Cap, the man he tried to kill, he would now be smashed to pulp.

Both men sagged, their chests heaving at the cool night air. Joe tapped Cap on the shoulder. "Thanks," he gulped. Cap nodded and a few moments later turned his horse and rode slowly back to camp. He made no reference to the attempt on his life, neither then nor when Johnny, with the herd safely on its way to the bedding ground, came into camp to report about twenty head of cattle lost.

When Johnny got the opportunity to get Joe to himself he said, "I saw what happened tonight, Cap saving you from certain death. I hope that's settled your grudge against Yankees. I figure Cap's paid you back your brother's life."

Joe made no comment but walked away.

# 7

THE following morning the herd settled down to its steady progress. The Hash Knife outfit, roused by the stampede, were more alert for Indians who, two days later, began to appear in greater numbers.

Cap sensed the alarm in his men for there was no way of telling how many Indians lay beyond the horizon or at the other side of a hill waiting for the signal to raid. Cap dealt patiently with the pleas for food for hungry squaw and starving papoose and deemed it wiser to give away a few head of cattle than risk greater loss now that they were deeper in Indian territory. Gradually the tension eased in Cap's men.

Apart from these incursions the days passed in the monotony of trail driving. Mile upon mile of seared brown grass stretched endlessly. Long horns clattered together as heads swung sideways; ankle joints cracked and hooves cut the ground sending choking dust skywards.

Cap longed for the end of the drive. The leads he had gained on the men he sought had made him restive for contact with Walt Mason and Rowdy Martin. He wanted to push the herd faster but to do so could be fatal to the price Johnny received. The cattle needed to be in good condition and to drive them too fast could mean loss in weight. So Cap curbed his desire for swift revenge and contented himself to the task on hand.

The Hash Knife moved out of Indian territory with no small measure of relief. Moving into Kansas brought its psychological fillip to the riders for they felt they were moving into the last phase of the drive to Abilene.

Their complacency was shattered when, during the noon stop a day into Kansas, two horsemen approached the camp. The Texans eyed them with some disdain for they could see by their ride and the way they handled their mounts that they were not much used to saddlework.

"Bloody farmers," muttered Jim Lovell voicing the thoughts of the rest of the Hash Knife men.

"Damned Unionists at that." Joe Durham hissed his contempt.

Both men wore old Army jackets over shirts tucked into belted trousers. Revolver butts protruded conspicuously and each man carried a rifle. Cap and Johnny laid their plates of stew down and climbed slowly to their feet.

Cap sensed the tension in the rest of the men. "All right, cool it," he said quietly but firmly so no one mistook his meaning. "I'll handle them."

He stepped forward with Johnny behind him as the two men pulled their horses to a halt. There was a tenseness in their bearded faces and while one surveyed the whole camp the other kept his eyes on Cap and Johnny.

He came straight to the point.

"Guess you're headin' fer Abilene; then find another way; we ain't having you through our land the other side of the next creek."

"We can't afford a detour," said Cap calmly.

"You've got to." The farmer went on to voice the surprise Cap had seen in his eyes when he had heard Cap's accent. "You ain't a Texan. Northerner?"

Cap nodded.

"Why the hell's a Northerner bossing a goddamned Texan drive? Ain't a Southern lover?" sneered the horseman.

Cap stiffened. His voice had a cold ring to it when he spoke. "I don't agree with some of their attitudes just as I don't like the one you're adopting now. Why can't you forget that bloody war and get on with living together. You want to know why I'm bossing this herd, well I'm here 'cos I'm a Northerner and the owner figured if we ran into the like of you you'd be more likely to talk sense with a Northerner

154

than with his Texas crew."

The man laughed but there was no humour in it, only contempt. "That ain't going to get you through. We ain't having cattle trample our crops and giving our cattle Texas fever. We ain't running the risk, so detour."

Cap's eyes narrowed. "Get your cattle out of the way."

"Like hell! We ain't obliging any goddamned Texan or a Northerner that rides with them."

Cap bristled. His hand flicked towards his Colt but he stopped when he saw the rifles had been levelled and fingers hitched at the triggers. "We're coming through," he said firmly.

"Then you'll meet a whole pack of trouble," warned the farmer. "Think it over and don't try it."

The two men backed their horses then suddenly wheeled and galloped away. Cap sensed the Hash Knife reaching for their guns.

"Leave them!" he rapped.

There were murmuring among the

Hash Knife men as they returned to their meal.

"You and I will take a look when we've finished our stew," said Cap as he picked up his plate.

An hour later Cap and Johnny saw a lone rider disappearing over the edge of a rise which they guessed led to the creek.

"Reckon we've been watched," Johnny commented.

When they halted their horses at the top of the rise they saw he was right. The lone rider had crossed the creek and was talking to a knot of ten men. They saw him gesticulate in their direction and in a moment all the men were running to their horses. They mounted and spaced themselves out about five yards from the bank of the creek.

"Looks as if they mean trouble," said Johnny.

"Figure we should pull out, bend the herd to the west?" queried Cap.

"I'm for through."

"Might lose some men and cattle. I ain't a Hash Knife man so it's up to you."

"Time's important. We go through."

"Right. One last peaceable attempt."

"You'll be lucky," commented Johnny as Cap put his horse down the slope to the creek through which a wide but shallow stream flowed.

"You letting us come through peaceable?" yelled Cap as he halted his horse.

"You had our word earlier; it ain't altered," came the sharp reply.

Johnny ran his eyes over the line of men on the opposite bank. Grim, determined faces looked across the water. Men with a cause, bent on defending it; they were not the type to give way. Do that now and you'd be doing it all the time. Stand firm now and future herds might take another route. Johnny had to admire their attitude. But he was just as determined to take the cattle through. And he knew Cap would not give way.

"We're coming through. One last chance to do it the right way," shouted Cap.

In reply two rifles came up sharply. Two shots crashed out. Bullets whined across the creek and spurted dust between the two horses. Frightened, the animals shied away from the disturbance but the skill of the riders kept them under control, wheeled them and sent them galloping up the slope. They had taken the message, next time there would be no warning shots.

The Hash Knife outfit came to their feet when Cap and Johnny rode up. They swung from their saddles and Cap explained the situation.

"There are ten armed men the other side of the creek determined to stop us. They may have some more to back them but I doubt it, I think they'd have tried to impress us with their full strength. The ground rises gently on this side then slopes long to the creek which is wide but shallow, not difficult to cross. We'll gentle the cattle to the

158

top of the rise then stampede them."
He glanced at Johnny who took over
the instructing.

"Keep the herd tight. Let them run
but under as much control as possible.
If any cattle stray forget them. We want
to be through these farmers fast. Josh,
you bring the remuda in close, the
horses will have to run with the herd.
Charlie, keep fairly close to the cattle
and when you hit the creek keep right
on going. Fox," he called to Honeyman
who was looking out of the back of
the wagon, "you'll have to put with a
bumpy ride."

"Sure, Johnny, I'll be all right. Can
handle a rifle from here, give them
bastards something to think about if
they give chase."

"Good man," called Cap.

Johnny quickly allocated the riders
their positions leaving himself and Cap
free to fit in as the situation demanded.

Satisfied, Cap glanced round them all.
"This is going to be rough but together
we'll get through. Any questions?" He

paused and when there were none he added, "Let's get 'em moving."

Men hurried to the horses they had selected and in a few minutes the herd was on the move again. Josh, riding back and forth along the right flank of the remuda, eased the horses nearer the herd. As Charlie set the chuck wagon in motion on the right point of the herd Fox checked his rifle.

Dust rose high in the still afternoon air, a signal to the waiting farmers who, as it advanced, knew their warning had been ignored.

As the herd moved towards the top of the rise Cap rode to every man checking that all was in order and offering a word of encouragement. He then signalled to Johnny and the two men rode ahead to the top of the rise where Charlie had halted the chuck wagon.

"Sure looks like a reception committee," observed Charlie indicating the farmers who lined the opposite bank.

"Wish we hadn't to stampede the cattle, Johnny," said Cap. "It'll run a bit of weight off, but we should get it back on before we get to Abilene."

When the leaders reached the top of the rise Cap ranged himself with one point rider while Johnny joined the other. Cap allowed the leaders to ease a short distance down the slope before he drew his Colt and loosed off a couple of shots across the front of the herd. Immediately the rest of the riders yelled and shouted, waved their Stetsons and rattled their rain slickers. Startled by the sudden and unexpected intrusion of sound the steers took off in a run. The cowboys urged them on and, once the whole herd was stampeding towards the creek, they concentrated on keeping the herd compact. Charlie held the chuck wagon's position until half the herd was past then he whipped the mules into a full gallop.

The herd thundered down the slope. The earth shook with the pound of the earth splitting hooves. A heaving sea of flesh and horn swept towards the farmers. Determination to hold their position broke in front of the frightening menace which hurled towards them. They had not calculated on this method of attack. Stopping men was one thing but halting a herd of stampeding cattle was another. The six men directly in the path of the longhorns broke in answer to the screaming fear of a horrible death which attacked their nerves. They raced out of the way of the onrushing steers.

"Drop the leaders!" yelled the farmer who had confronted Cap. "Drop the leaders!"

The herd hit the creek. Water splashed high as the steers tore on. Farmers raised their rifles but their shots were wide for, even as they fired, their horses, frightened by the thundering noise, were turning away. Six of the farmers, realizing they had made a mistake by staying mounted, quickly dropped to the ground.

Rifles blazed and, as they reached the bank, two lead steers fell. But it was too late. There was little effect on the stampede and the cattle rushed onwards. The rest of the leaders were through and the herd would follow. Cap and Johnny broke away from the point riders on either side of the herd leaving them to keep the leaders in their run. Their shots diverted the attention of the farmers trying to get a perfect sighting on the riders alongside the herd.

The chuck wagon hit the creek at a bouncing run but Charlie kept the mules moving. Water and stones churned beneath the wheels. Then it was over and Charlie was urging the animals to keep up their pace. Bullets clipped through the canvas covering and Charlie felt a searing pain in the top of his left arm. Rifles crashed ahead of him. He held on. Then he was through the farmers and from the rear of the chuck wagon Fox's rifle sent them diving for cover.

Johnny wheeling and turning his horse so as not to present an easy target, watched Charlie anxiously but as the wagon swept past him he saw that Charlie was in full control. A bullet clipped his saddle bringing the Hash Knife foreman's concentration back to the farmers. He saw a man moving his rifle in line with a galloping rider but before the farmer could fire Johnny's bullet sent him crashing to the ground. The farmers kept up their fusillade of fire but, with dust now obscuring good vision and the spread of the stampeding cattle and riders, their efforts were useless.

The drag men urged the last of the cattle over the creek. Johnny and Cap kept up their covering fire and then wheeled their horses behind them. A few moments later the two men dropped further back, steadied their mounts and turned in their saddles to assess the situation.

The farmers weren't bothering to get their horses for pursuit. They knew their task was hopeless. The cattle they had hoped to turn were across, running fast through their land. Johnny and Cap grinned at each other and put their animals into a steady gallop after the herd. The way should be clear for the final miles to Abilene.

# 8

CAP watched Abilene rise from the flatness. A cold excitement which brought a tenseness gripped him. Two men whom he sought were somewhere in that town. He had only Jess Sharp's word. Walt Mason and Rowdy Martin may have moved on but Cap had a feeling that that was not so. He sensed that the men were still there and would soon be facing the justice of his Colt.

The cattle eased their way over the last few miles, feeding on the lush grass on the approach to the cattle pens beside the railroad on the edge of Abilene.

Johnny was about to leave the herd and ride into town to put through a sale when a bunch of riders approached.

"Howdy." The leader, a broad shouldered weighty man, smiled his greeting. "Mighty fine looking cattle you've got. Texas?"

Johnny nodded. "Hash Knife. Johnny Hines, foreman. Cap Millet, here, trail boss."

"John Charleston." The big man introduced himself. "Cattle buyer for the Eastern Meat Company. Like to have a closer look at your herd." His last remark was addressed to Cap.

"Deal with Johnny," replied Cap. "I only brought the herd north."

The man nodded and turned to Johnny. Within the hour the herd had been examined, a price agreed, a note to the bank signed and passed to Johnny and the herd handed over to the men who had arrived with John Charleston.

Pleased with the price and the swiftness of the deal, Johnny told the men that he would pay them off in town, then as far as he was concerned the drive was over, they were released but he hoped he would see them all back on the Hash Knife.

167

Relieved to be rid of the cattle and the responsibilities of the trail drive, with no more dust to chew, no more Indians, stampedes and farmers to contend with, the Hash Knife cowboys rode into Abilene determined to have some end of the trail celebrations before setting off for Texas.

But Clint Forbes and Joe Durham had some unfinished business to attend to before that celebration.

As the band of men broke up after being paid off, Clint and Joe kept to themselves and, while seeming to follow the others to the saloon, kept their eyes on Cap, Wade and Josh. The three men talked in earnest for a while then Josh gathered the reins of their three horses and made his way towards the livery stable at the east end of town.

Cap and Wade went into a store next to the bank and Clint and Joe positioned themselves outside the saloon to await their reappearance. Five minutes later Cap and Wade emerged from the store and walked briskly along the sidewalk.

As Clint and Joe pushed themselves from the chairs they had occupied, Johnny came out of the bank. His preoccupation with his thoughts was interrupted when his glance took in the street ahead of him and he saw Clint and Joe were following Cap and Wade. So the Hash Knife men still nurtured the feeling for revenge. Johnny keeping his distance followed.

Cap and Wade turned into a side street which was flanked by a row of one-storeyed houses. Reaching the fifth one they stopped. Cap spoke briefly to Wade and left him standing by the gate. Cap walked to the veranda, climbed the four steps and knocked on the front door.

Taking in the situation from the end of the street, Clint and Joe crossed the main street and took up a position from which they could see the house. Johnny, observing the actions of the Hash Knife hands, held back and kept them under surveillance from outside a store.

Cap waited impatiently for an answer

to his knock. He tried to get a grip on his feelings, this was no way to approach a showdown. His fists clenched and he became aware of the sweat on his palms. He rubbed them on his trousers, annoyed that some of the ice coldness which had dominated his thoughts for so long had been erroded. What was wrong with him? He forced some steadiness back to his mind but that received a jolt when the door was opened by a pretty young woman. Her open, friendly face smiled a greeting and posed a query as to what he wanted.

"Good day, ma'am," said Cap, touching the brim of his Stetson with his right forefinger. "I'm looking for Walt Mason, told me in the store that I could find him here."

"That's right," she smiled. "You're lucky, my husband was just about to go out. Who wants him?"

Cap's mind pounded. Husband! This was something he hadn't thought about. Mason married. A pretty gal too. A widow in a few minutes. Cap's stomach knotted. He felt sick. His revenge was going to sweep into another life. And a young wife's at that. What would she say if she knew her husband was a rapist and a murderer? What should . . .

His tumbling thoughts were broken by a repetition of her question.

"Er, sorry, ma'am. Cap Millet."

She nodded and turned away from the door. A few moment later she was back, "Come in," she said.

Cap followed her into a sparsely furnished but neat room and almost at the same instant a young man, no more than twenty-four Cap figured, appeared.

He smiled and held out his hand. "Walt Mason. Cap Millet, Laura tells me. Pleased to know you."

Cap took the firm, friendly grip and saw a pleasant face, one which seemed to have pushed the horrors of war into the background in order to get on with living. Could this man have raped and murdered Kathy? It seemed incredible standing here in the peace of his home with his pretty wife beside him, but war did strange things to men, turned them into beings even they themselves would not recognize afterwards.

But no matter, if this man had committed the crime he must pay. Cap jolted his racing thought to a stop as he realized that two people were looking at him, waiting to know the nature of his business.

"Do you know Jess Sharp, Pete Carter and Rowdy Martin?" Cap put the question without explanation.

Walt smiled, "Army buddies of mine. I haven't heard of Jess or Pete since we split up after the war. Jess said he was thinking of signing on. Rowdy and I teamed up, we worked around a few ranches then decided to come to Abilene, work hard, save hard and buy a spread of our own." His voice tailed off and his smile had been replaced by a sadness.

"Rowdy still around?" asked Cap.

"Got caught in a gunfight in town. No concern of his, just in the way. He got killed and the bastards who caused it weren't even hurt."

"Sorry about that," said Cap.

Walt pushed the thoughts of his friend from his mind and again queried Cap's reason for coming.

"I believe you four, during the retreat, buried a woman outside her house."

Walt and Laura exchanged glances of surprise that this incident, long banished to the mind's subconscious, should now be brought back by this stranger. Cap realized that Laura knew something, but how much?

Walt nodded. "Yes we did. But why do you want to know?"

"She was my wife!"

The announcement stunned both husband and wife. Laura gasped, her eyes widened. Walt stared at Cap unable to speak for a moment. Cap watched him carefully. Was it the unexpected or the thought of retribution at the hands of the dead woman's husband that held his tongue?

"I've looked for you since the end of

the war. I want to know how she died."
Cap broke the silence.

"She was dead when we found her."

Anger seethed in Cap. This is what he had expected to hear. He tightened the grip on his feelings. He must hear Mason out.

"Tell me about it."

Walt looked at his wife. "Make us some coffee, Laura." He turned her gently and opened the door. As he closed it again he indicated a chair to Cap. "Laura knows we buried someone but she doesn't know the whole story. It's not pretty. How much do you want to know?"

"All of it. Hold nothing back. I've searched for four years."

Walt licked his lips, not relishing the recall. "We were running. All hell had been let loose and not even the rain and the mud dampened the things which went on. We four, tired, hungry, soaked, came to this house. It seemed like a haven amongst the horror if only for a few minutes. We could escape the rain, ease our weariness, maybe even find some food. We went in. There was a strange atmosphere, can't tell you what it was, but it was foreboding, as if trouble was reaching out to us. We all felt it. Rowdy wanted to get out there and then, I was inclined the same way but the gnawing at our stomachs was powerful. We searched for food. There was nothing downstairs but we figured someone might have hidden something so we searched some more."

Walt's voice faltered as if he didn't want to relate any more but he forced himself to go on. "I found her in the main bedroom. It was in a turmoil. There had obviously been a violent struggle but she had lost. She lay spreadeagled on the bed, naked." He glanced at Cap but Cap was unaware of him, he was hearing the words and seeing that room in which he had known and loved Kathy. Walt knew he must go on. "Her clothes, torn and ripped were scattered all around, it was obvious that they had been torn from her violently. She must have been viciously used but the horror had not ended there. There was blood everywhere. I've seen bayonet slits and some bastard had inserted one into her and slit her upwards."

The words thundered in Cap's mind. The hell of Kathy's death stormed at him. His eyes brought Walt back into focus. This bloody rapist could sit here and describe it, he had nerve hoping to push the blame on to someone else. Cap's hand moved towards his gun but it never reached it for the door opened as Laura looked in.

"Don't forget the cross and chain, dear," she said.

"Thanks," replied Walt. "I had forgotten it." He got to his feet, crossed the room to a chest of drawers and opened the top one. He fumbled inside and when he turned round he held up a delicate chain from which hung a small cross. "I guess this is rightly yours," he said.

Cap stared at the cross. His thoughts

tumbled in confusion.

"I found it on the floor, guess it must have been torn from her neck by the person who attacked her. I don't know why I picked it up, reckon I figured on putting it with her when we buried her, you see we couldn't leave her there not like that, but in our haste to be away I must have forgotten I had it in my pocket. I've kept it ever since. But you take it, it's yours."

Cap reached out and took the cross. He stared at it for a long moment then looked up at Walt.

"Thanks for telling me," he said quietly. His mind had gone ice cold again. "And thanks for burying Kathy." He turned to the door. "Tell your wife thanks for the coffee. I'm sorry I can't stay to have it." He pulled open the door and before Walt could speak he was across the hall and outside. Walt stared in amazement at the swiftness of Cap's leaving.

Cap swung out of the gate and his strides lengthened towards the main street. Wade hurried and fell in beside him.

"You done for him, boss? I heard no shot."

"Married. And Rowdy Martin's dead."

"That his wife who came to the door? Pretty little thing."

Cap nodded, his face grim. Wade had seen that look before and knew it best to say no more. So his boss had gone soft at the finish, sight of a pretty girl had stopped him. Four years searching and now this, no revenge, nothing. But what did it matter to Wade? It was his boss's affair.

When Clint and Joe saw Cap come out of the house they moved out of sight. Johnny did likewise when he saw Cap and Wade turn the corner and start along the main street. He held his preoccupation with the goods in the store until they had passed and he had seen that Clint and Joe were following.

The two Hash Knife men quickened their pace when they saw Cap and Wade

178

turn into the livery stable. They moved close to the door where they were able to hear what was going on inside.

Johnny saw their hand hover near their Colts. The three men in the livery stable, taken completely by surprise would be easy targets unless he acted quickly. He eased his Colt from its holster and raced quickly but silently towards the stable. "Ease it, you two," he hissed. Startled the two men glanced round.

"Hold it, Johnny," whispered Clint.

As Johnny came nearer voices reached them from the stable.

"Hi, Mister Cap. Horses just about ready. You done for them two white fellas? Hope so. I'll be mighty glad to get out of here. Want no trouble with that Hash Knife outfit."

"One horse won't be needed, Josh." Cap's voice was cold.

"What you mean, boss?" asked a surprised Josh. "If you're staying, what about Wade and me?"

"I ain't staying, Josh. You are!" As he

spoke he held up the chain and cross.

Josh's eyes widened into whiteness. An icy hand gripped him.

"Yours, Josh. The one Kathy gave you."

"That's right boss." Josh forced a laugh. "Didn't know you had it."

"Hadn't until a few minutes ago. Walt Mason gave it to me. He picked it up in the room where he found Kathy's mutilated body." He watched Josh carefully, willing him to go for his gun. He saw terror coming into the negro's eyes as he realized Cap knew the truth. "Walt Mason figured it had been torn from Kathy's neck by the man who raped and killed her, but you and I know better, don't we, Josh? She tore it from your neck as she fought with you. Didn't she, Josh? And when you finished raping her you had to use a bayonet." Cap's voice rose. "You bloody, black bastard, shooting's too good for you . . . "

"I had no bayonet!" yelled Josh, sweat breaking out on his forehead as he cringed from the truth. "I had no bayonet! It was Wade! He came back egged me on saying she was a Southerner who had no time for blacks or Northerners. We were . . . "

"Shut it, nigger!" Wade's voice rapped harshly. His gun was out of its holster digging into Cap's side, "Don't try anything," he warned.

Cap's mind reeled under the disclosure. Black and white as guilty as each other, men whom he had befriended, men who had ridden on a trail of revenge and who would have let him take vengeance on innocent men, to remain in the clear. Black, white, Northerner, Southerner, what the hell did it matter? All men were alike — good or bad.

Josh was regaining his confidence with Cap at the mercy of Wade's gun. He grinned then laughed loudly. "Oh, we did it, boss. Fed up of the airs and graces of Miss Kathy and then Mrs Cap."

"That's not true," yelled Cap. "She was kind to you."

"A no good Southerner, and you were as bad for marrying a Southerner, that's what Wade said. We'd make her pay for you both, well we sure did." There was a wild look in Josh's eyes as he recalled that day over four years ago. "She sure was good, Mister Cap, she sure was."

"Shut up, damn you, shut up!" yelled Wade angered by Josh's revelations.

Cap felt the gun ease in his side as Wade yelled at Josh. He had to act, he had to take a risk or be shot down in cold blood. These two would show no mercy, he knew too much, if they let him off now they knew they would be looking over their shoulders all their lives.

"What you scared of Wade?" mocked Josh. "Scared of remembering what she looked like when you used the bayonet?"

"Shut up," hissed Wade.

The gun swung away from Cap's side as Wade's attention was diverted by Josh's mockery.

Cap seized the moment. He swung

sharply round knocking Wade's arm and propelling himself into his body. Wade lost his balance and crashed to the floor. Before Josh realized what was happening Cap kept moving and flung himself into one of the stalls. He rolled over and came up into a crouching position behind the protection of the partition.

Josh and Wade dived for the cover of some straw near the door. "We've still got him," yelled Wade. "He can't get . . ."

"Like hell you have!" the words boomed behind them as the stable door crashed open. Josh and Wade swung round in alarm. Their eyes widened in disbelief as Clint and Joe strode in with Colts in hand backed up by Johnny. Clint and Joe waited a fraction of a second to see Wade and Josh start to raise their guns. The Hash Knife men made no mistake, they had the advantage — coolness in the element of surprise. Bullets ripped into the two men pitching them back into the straw.

"All right, Cap, we got the bastards," called Clint.

Johnny grinned to himself as he saw Clint and Joe slip their guns back into their holsters.

Cap rose slowly from the stall. He still held his Colt and there was suspicion in his eyes. Then he saw the guns were back in their holsters.

"What . . . " he started.

"We heard it all," explained Clint. "Oh we'd come gunning for the three of you but Johnny got the drop on us. Then we heard the whole story and Johnny knew these two deserved it. Sorry about what happened way back."

"Thanks," said Cap. He eyed Joe Durham. "I'm still a Yankee."

"Sure, but not a bad one at that," grinned Joe and held out his hand.

Cap took the firm grip.

"I reckon there's good and bad in all," said Clint. "Remember telling me that about the blacks that day back at the Red well I guess I see you're right."

184

Cap grinned and slapped Clint on the shoulder.

"Well I guess I've heard it all now," laughed Johnny. "What you going to do now, Cap?"

"I've nowhere particular to go so if you don't mind I'll ride back to the Hash Knife with you. And don't get alarmed, I'm not coming for my old job, just going to report to Frank what a good crew he's got before I head West."

## THE END

*Other titles in the*
*Linford Western Library:*

## TOP HAND
### Wade Everett

The Broken T was big. But no ranch is big enough to let a man hide from himself.

## GUN WOLVES OF LOBO BASIN
### Lee Floren

The Feud was a blood debt. When Smoke Talbot found the outlaws who gunned down his folks he aimed to nail their hide to the barn door.

## SHOTGUN SHARKEY
### Marshall Grover

The westbound coach carrying the indomitable Larry and Stretch headed for a shooting showdown.